D0593157

Lila
The Sign of the Elven Queen

DEDICATION

This book is dedicated to my friend, Lila, and my niece, Samantha. One day the two of you will be grown women, but not yet, and I am delighted to have known both of you during the "not yet" part of your lives. I also dedicate this book to my mother who had the good sense to read me *Winnie the Pooh* on many occasions. That bear had a great deal of wisdom, and thanks for sharing it with me when I was "not yet" and needed it most. I love you all!

—Mark J. Grant

Requests for permission to make copies of any
part of the work should be submitted online to
info@mascotbooks.com or mailed to:

Mascot Books
560 Herndon Parkway #120
Herndon, VA 20170.

Library of Congress Control Number: 2013943802

ISBN-10: 1-620863-57-X
ISBN-13: 978-1-620863-57-2
CPSIA Code: PRB0613A

Layout and illustrations by Danny Moore

Printed in the United States of America

www.mascotbooks.com

LILA

THE SIGN OF THE ELVEN QUEEN

By Mark J. Grant

TABLE OF CONTENTS

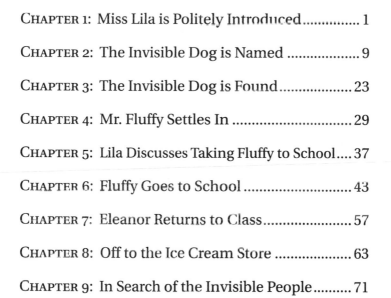

CHAPTER 1: Miss Lila is Politely Introduced 1

CHAPTER 2: The Invisible Dog is Named 9

CHAPTER 3: The Invisible Dog is Found 23

CHAPTER 4: Mr. Fluffy Settles In 29

CHAPTER 5: Lila Discusses Taking Fluffy to School 37

CHAPTER 6: Fluffy Goes to School 43

CHAPTER 7: Eleanor Returns to Class 57

CHAPTER 8: Off to the Ice Cream Store 63

CHAPTER 9: In Search of the Invisible People 71

CHAPTER 10: The Search Continues 85

CHAPTER 11: And What Next 105

CHAPTER 12: Next Arrives 113

CHAPTER 13: What Comes After Next 127

CHAPTER 14: Old Dogs and New Tricks................... 139

CHAPTER 15: The Morning Changed Nothing........ 149

CHAPTER 16: An Answer.. 159

CHAPTER 17: Almost There 179

CHAPTER 18: Boulder I, Parliament House............. 189

CHAPTER 19: Lila is Almost Seven 205

CHAPTER 20: The Big Day Arrives........................... 209

CHAPTER 21: The Way In 213

CHAPTER 22: Boulder II, Castlerock 219

CHAPTER 23: Dreams Come True............................ 225

CHAPTER 1

MISS LILA IS POLITELY INTRODUCED

Lila had learned to be polite at a very early age. She was six years old now and she recalled that her mother had given her instructions about being polite more than once, but she could not remember exactly when her instructions started. She seemed to think that it began at about three, but she was not quite certain. Three was a half a life ago and it was similar to being sixty and trying to remember something that took place when you were thirty, but she wasn't exactly sure about that either, being nowhere close to sixty.

To be more precise Lila had only learned about sixty recently, and it seemed such a large number

that there must not be many numbers past sixty and if there were they couldn't be that important. She knew that adults frequently mentioned numbers bigger than sixty but she could not imagine what they were for or why anyone would care. Sixty was quite large enough, thank you, and it hurt her head to try to imagine any numbers that might exceed that one.

Five dolls was something she could understand, and perhaps ten or fifteen might be useful as you wanted to have different conversations with your special friends, but it would take many days to converse with sixty dolls so that she dismissed that amount of dolls out of hand. Lila had met a girl once at school that claimed to have zillions of dolls bought by her father who worked in some street with really high walls or something, but she saw no value in any of it and anyway, she didn't believe her because so many dolls would not allow for any space for people or cats or dogs and everyone knew that parents and children and pets must have someplace to eat and sleep. Dolls were important, of course, but people and animals more so, of that much she was certain.

Lila had asked her mother about this once. "Mama, why can dolls sleep anywhere, but people all

sleep in beds and our animals all seem to have places that they have chosen for sleeping?" Her mother had explained that people prefer comfy places, and floors and the like are not comfy, while the cats and dogs chose sleeping places for reasons that people could not understand. She got the first part of this as she had personally tried to sleep on the floor just to see what it was like, and it was not nearly as comfy as her bed. Floors were useful for walking or perhaps crawling when you were much younger but she was in agreement with her mother that floors were not so much for sleeping.

Now some of her dolls did sleep with her on her bed. This was one of the decisions she made at night right before she went to sleep: which dolls would accompany her to bed. Every night was different, she was one day older after all, and so different choices had to be made, but this just seemed to be the way of growing older. Of course, it also partially depended upon which dolls behaved during the day and which ones had provided some sort of amusing conversation. Dolls, just like her mother and father, could be quite cranky at times, and so on those days they were not allowed to sleep with her. Lila had decided that she had to put up with cranky parents because, what could be done, but that her dolls were a different matter. It seemed quite unfair really. Her parents tried to control her all of the time but she had no control over them, and the difference between being a child and being a parent seemed quite distinct, but if that was the way it was, at least she could control her dolls.

Now Lila was neither a big six nor a little six but she was certainly a very big-eyed six. She had the largest eyes of any six-year-old in the city in which she lived, which was New York City. There are many people that lived there of course, and you could wander from Manhattan to Brooklyn and look around, but she could claim the biggest eyes. It was uncertain how this took place as both her father and mother had normal sized eyes, but not Miss Lila. It may have been that God decided she should see better than most, or that she should be set aside as a very particular little girl. We will never really know the reason of course, but the largest eyes on this side of the Hudson River are what she had and of that there is no question.

They were not the bug-kind of eyes nor were they the protruding type, but just eyes like saucers that she used for the tea parties that she had with

her dolls. Her mother favored fancy blue tea cups and saucers and Lila liked the white ones with all of the interesting scrolls that she thought might mean something, kind of like the writing that her mother kept trying to get her to understand. It was just that the books with writing but without pictures seemed so dull and commonplace, that it was hard to pay attention to them, especially when the dolls wanted to have a conversation.

Each doll had a distinct personality. This was because each one reminded her of some person that either she knew or wanted to know, such as some of the people in TV shows or some of the singers that seemed quite beautiful to her. She had no idea how one became a singer actually or even how one got to be on a TV show, but they both seemed so glamorous that she supposed some of her dolls must be relatives of these people. This did bring about a sort of problem for Lila. She had asked her mother many times about this, but just who was a relative and who was not was quite unclear. There was Mama's mother and Papa's mother and she understood that they were her parent's mothers like Mama was her mother.

How one became a mother though was a great

uncertainty, though Mama had said she would explain when she was a few years older. Lila was actually quite glad of this because even though she was a very inquisitive child, she had this feeling in her tummy that the explanation would be long and complicated and make her head hurt just like when she considered numbers larger than sixty. Lila knew it had something to do with men and women and the difference between them, but as far as she was concerned, Mama was her parent and Papa was her parent and that was quite enough to know, thank you.

Now Lila's family had two cats. One was a normal enough looking furball, but the other was very strange and particular. His face was odd, his smile was lopsided, and when he smiled, which was rarely, his fur stuck out in a very peculiar manner. This cat did not look at all like the cats in the cat books that Mama read to her, so it was a question of either having a strange cat, or that Mama was showing her strange books. It took Lila almost three days to decide this issue and it was somewhat painful because Mama had told her that the cat book cats were perfectly normal. She finally concluded that Mama would not mislead her so that it must be her cat who was not quite like other cats. Lila did not love this cat any less however, as one might imagine, but accepted him for who he was and as a member of the family. This decision was also useful at school.

Some of the girls at her school, never mind the boys because they didn't really count, were also a little strange and they reminded her of her cat. She at first thought to stay away from the strange girls, but then after the cat decision, she realized that they might be her friends after all, even though they were not quite like her. She was a well-liked child, and Lila was often invited for sleepovers and here was where she learned why some of her new acquaintances were similar to her cat. It was because the parents were similar to the cat.

Lila then concluded that odd parents make odd children but that being strange was not so bad in itself—they were just different, which could be either good or bad. The trouble of course, was figuring out which was which, but as long as they were nice and fed her and she was not scared, then she felt that they were fine. This was a big revelation for Lila—strange could be fine and the people that were strange could be fine, just in a different way from Mama and Papa and her. She was relieved, finally, that she got this

settled in her mind because she was afraid it was going to be another some number over sixty kind of problem.

Chapter 2

The Invisible Dog is Named

Lila had always wanted a dog. This was mostly the fault of Uncle Mark, who was really not her uncle as her father had explained, but it didn't seem to matter. Uncles were always nice and kind, as everyone knows who is anybody, so that "not really her uncle" seemed to be a matter of pretend which was fine because she liked pretend quite well. A pretend uncle then, not the brother of Mama or Papa, fit in somehow to her family but she couldn't quite make it out. Explanations had been given and questions had been asked but not being anyone's brother seemed to make no difference. What Uncle Mark was though, was the owner of three remarkable things and this

made him quite special.

The first was his boat. It was large enough to be out on the ocean, which she had done with her parents, and there was always the hope of seeing a porpoise, or a whale or some fish that she had never seen. Lila loved the ocean and to be out on it in Uncle Mark's boat was something even better than pretend because she could smell the salt in the air and watch the world go by in a way that she could not do in her apartment in New York. This was not pretend at all, she decided, but something really, really special.

Lila loved Uncle Mark's boat. She was ready to go out on it anytime he asked her. She even thought of his boat when the days were cold and grey and then she said to herself, "I would rather be on Uncle Mark's boat, and Papa should call him so we can do just that."

She had asked often enough but Papa kept saying Uncle Mark was busy doing something with work, whatever that is, but she supposed it was like homework. Why Uncle Mark would rather be doing work instead of out on his boat was something that she could not understand at all. Perhaps someone was making Uncle Mark do this work, like her teachers made her do homework, so she forgave

Uncle Mark on the basis that he had no choice and should therefore not be blamed. The boat, however, was not the best of what Uncle Mark owned, because those two places were reserved for Princess and Mr. Trooper.

These two dogs, Lila was told, were Aussies. She was not exactly sure what an Aussie was but it was clear that it was some kind of dog. She had noted that dogs came in different sizes and were of different colors so she supposed that an Aussie dog was different than other dogs such as collie dogs, or bulldogs, though the latter looked nothing like any bull she had seen in her picture books.

Regardless, Princess and Mr. Trooper were her favorite dogs and not just because they went with her on the boat. They were both so fluffy and excited to see her, even though they could not have been as excited to see her as she was excited to see them. When they saw her they jumped in the air, and Lila supposed that this was their way of greeting her, so she jumped in the air back. Mama had said that one should always be polite and greet people the way she was greeted, and she saw no reason at all why this did not apply to dogs. She was sure in fact, that it

did apply to dogs, because neither Mama nor Papa objected when she jumped in the air back and so it must be fine.

The dogs were also quite special in another way too, Uncle Mark had explained to her. They were rescue dogs. What a nice thing it must be to rescue people or dogs, she supposed, which also made Uncle Mark quite special in her eyes because he had done just that. What she could not figure out, however, is why they needed to be rescued. What kind of people would abandon their dogs?

Her parents had told her often enough that some people in the world were not nice and that they should be avoided, but to leave one's dogs behind was like one of those math problems at school which was just not explainable no matter how hard she tried to understand it. She could see that two plus two made four but when it got to twenty plus thirty plus forty, it all came back to the numbers over sixty problem which caused her to wince and shut her eyes and get lost. It all must add up to something, though she was not sure what.

Lila often thought that simple things were better things, as they could be understood with ease, and

why parents and teachers needed to make simple things complicated was something that she had not yet figured out. It was clear that one Princess and one Mr. Trooper made two and that was quite enough for today. Besides that, when she was with the dogs, they all made three and while something might be better than having the three of them together, she could not imagine what that might be.

Lila often spoke with the two dogs, her parents noted, and while they did not respond back in English, there was never a doubt that they were communicating in a very pleasant manner. Lila talked and the dogs barked and the dogs barked and Lila talked and everyone got along just fine. Lila also noted that Uncle Mark gave the dogs treats, and she first wondered and then asked if she could not be the giver of treats—when approved by Uncle Mark, of course.

She did not know her parents' ages or Uncle Mark's age for that matter, but she did know they were all adults, which is anyone who is not a child, and so one must get approval for these sorts of things otherwise trouble could be found. For sure she did not want what came with trouble to disturb her very pleasant afternoon with the dogs, so she took the easy way out. This was just the way of things. Better to ask then do rather than the other way around, which generally brought the trouble and then some sort of punishment that came along with it.

Lila had no use for sitting alone in her room or sitting in some kind of "time out." Time seemed to go along anyway, or so said the clock in the hallway, but it was the words that her parents used and so she supposed that it must have some meaning. She never asked about it, however, because she didn't want to know any more than she had to about trouble and punishments, and so refused to inquire about the subject. "It is better not to know," she told herself, "because knowing could make it all worse." And she just hated worse.

Sitting in her room one afternoon on a very yucky day, she decided that she missed Mr. Trooper and Princess. She had thought this from time to time but it always seemed to become more acute on the gloomy days when the sun was not out and it was raining or snowing or the sky was doing something unpleasant, whatever it was called. Perched on her bed, surrounded by various dolls that had behaved

that day, she decided that she wanted a dog of her own. This was a bit of a problem, she knew, because she already had two cats and she lived in an apartment and she could not visualize Papa allowing another animal in the house. She also suspected that her building might not allow dogs and so she was feeling quite gloomy and she hated feeling gloomy. There is nothing good about gloomy, she had long ago concluded, because smiling was not possible when gloomy and it was like living under a big wet blanket. One therefore had to climb out of gloomy, carefully of course so as not to get too wet, and then set about whatever it was that returned you to a happy feeling.

She looked about her room and nothing seemed to provide that much happiness at this moment. She surveyed her dolls, her toys and even other objects that might work if she entered her pretend mode, which was always a comfy place to be. She thought and she thought and then it came to her, "Why can't I have a pretend dog?" she said aloud and at just that very moment she had thrown off the gloomy and found herself out from underneath the wet blanket. She was now excited and shaking with anticipation as Papa would be home soon and she couldn't wait to ask his permission for her pretend dog, her invisible dog, that no one would see but her.

As she sat there and thought about how she should approach Papa to get what she wanted, it occurred to her that she would have to do certain things with her invisible dog so that he was happy. She would have to feed him, but then feeding, she knew, also led to pooping, and what was she to do about that? This could be a problem. Invisible dogs could eat invisible food and so that was not so tough, but the pooping was another matter entirely. Mama, she knew, would be furious if a dog pooped in the living room, whether invisible or not. It might smell, and even worse, someone would have to clean up after the dog and Lila wanted nothing to do with that. She then frowned and tried to think how it might work and the furrows on her forehead, usually as smooth as her red cheeks, deepened as she thought about it some more.

This was a number over sixty kind of problem and it just made her tired to even think about any answers. She had never heard of a dog using the toilet, she had never seen a picture of anything like that in one of her books, but then that might be because somehow pictures of people on toilets were not quite polite so

that dogs sitting on toilets might not be polite either, and her mama always told her that a young woman must always be polite. She then smiled and giggled out loud because she knew her new invisible dog friend would also be polite, there was to be no other way of course, and he would use the toilet like she did and so the problem was solved and kicked under her bed, which was what she did with difficult problems after they had been sorted out.

Now the problem was no longer a problem and it was squarely under the bed and it would not bother her anymore. This is why she liked her bed so much. Not only was it more comfy than sleeping on the floor, but it could be used just like a wastebasket to throw difficulties underneath, which was a very useful sort of bed to own after all. She just loved her bed.

She heard the key go into the lock, she heard the tumbler make that lock sound and she rushed from her room. This was not a skipping thing or a grown-up walking kind of thing, but a full-blown rush to the front door and into the arms of her papa. "Papa, Papa, Papa," she cried because she knew this delighted him and she felt just that way in any event.

"Papa, you must listen to me, you have to say

'yes,' you just must say 'yes,' and please do not tell me anything at all but 'yes.' Okay?"

"Lila," he laughed with great merriment, "I do not even know the question yet. How can I say 'yes' if you have not even told me what you want? What if you ask me some impossible thing like having dinner tonight in Paris, France, and I have already said 'yes' and then how am I going to be able to give you what you want? You could be terribly disappointed if I give you an answer first, so you must tell me the question and then I shall see about saying yes. Okay?"

"Yes, yes, okay, okay, so here is what I want which is an invisible dog to play with me in the house. Don't say 'no,' you must not say 'no' and I will feed him, brush him and train him to use the toilet just like me. Okay? Okay? Okay?"

Papa winced and his mind rushed about like Lila had rushed into his arms. What did one do with an invisible dog? Where did one get invisible food or an invisible brush? Should he explain that dogs did not use toilets, and how would he explain it and what if the invisible dog was using the toilet when he needed to shave or wanted to take a shower, and then Lila might become upset that he was not being polite to this invisible dog, and what was the dog's name anyway?

"Well, Lila, have you discussed this with your mother?" Papa asked. "You and your mother are home together, you know, and I am at work. Don't you think we should discuss this with her first?" This was the famous put-off play of Papa's that she knew only too well. Her father engaged in it as often as her mother, but she had heard it so many times before that she already had the answer. She said she was quite sure, quite certain, that Mama would just be oh so delighted to have an invisible dog in the house because it would protect them both from any ogres or things of that nature that might come around. She was not quite sure, it must be said, what an ogre was, but she knew enough that no one wanted any ogres to show up—unless invited of course. *Invited ogres must be okay,* she thought, *as anyone or thing that was invited over was meant to be there.*

It was just at this moment that her mother entered the room. "Er, um. Hello, darling," Papa smiled and said to Mama. "And how was your day?"

"Fine, all good, I took Lila to school, stopped at the grocery store and saw the cutest dress at the department store but did not buy it and will not until it goes on sale because I want to save you the money," she said glibly. She was Lila's mother after all and had her own designs on Papa which were necessary from time to time, as men were such funny creatures and had to be handled quite carefully if you wanted to get what you wanted—which she always did.

Papa grinned and mumbled something which no one could quite hear and then he inquired if Lila had told her anything about any invisible dog and, if so, what was its name. This was the second time that Papa had asked about the name of the dog and she had not fully considered this question yet.

"What was the name of this dog going to be?" she asked herself. She did not want a common name of course, or some name of one of those show-off boys in school—she certainly did not want that. Lila hurriedly wrote off any name of any boy that she could think of because her invisible dog needed a proper name and a lovely name and one that described him right down to his paws and his fluffy tail and then it came to her: The dog would be named "Fluffy." Here was the perfect name and one that she could share with her dolls and her other female friends when

asked, and one that was perfectly suited for her new four-legged friend. So Fluffy it was and this she quickly announced so that there would be no further confusion, and she smiled ever so sweetly at Papa and announced, "The dog's name is Fluffy."

ICELAND

Chapter 3
The Invisible Dog is Found

There was a problem. Lila's parents had given the basic approval for the invisible dog and thought it quite kind of Lila not to ask for a real one that did need to be fed, brushed and taken outside to take care of business. The cats would not be furious, the rugs would not be the object of puppy mistakes and the lack of the inevitable trips outside with the dog in the cold and snow would be a blessing. The invisible dog seemed to be quite manageable and if it would make Lila happy, well then, that was a good thing. It might even settle her down some past the bouts of great excitement, and the occasional moments when she laid on the floor and beat her fists against the wood in exasperation.

Yes, Lila was a spirited child and while mostly in good humor, there were "those" moments that also seemed to come with being a normal girl of six. It was generally not clear what exactly to do when a young girl turned red in the face, could not speak because no words would come out and then, in utter frustration, threw herself on the quite uncomfortable floor and took out her problems on the wood that was beneath her. The floor was never harmed of course, being of a resilient nature, but poor Lila's fists were not well designed for the task. The tears running down her face were not things of beauty or even something any parents would want to endure more than is necessary as part of the childhood experience. "Yes, yes the dog can be found and brought home," said Papa, but where does one find an invisible dog was the question.

Lila's parents had discussed this several times during the next few days after they had agreed to let the invisible dog in the house, but it was only after Lila's mother quipped that, "Invisible dogs are found at invisible pet stores," that a plan began to come together. Papa would take Lila to a pet store a few blocks away, and Fluffy would be found waiting for her just outside. Then, if necessary, they could go inside and get the invisible food, the invisible brush and any invisible treats that might be necessary to ensure Fluffy's well-being. That was the plan anyway, because with children, as everyone knows, the best laid plans sometimes go far, far astray.

The next morning was Saturday morning, always a good day for visiting pet stores, toy stores or even museums where hopefully a young lady might learn something of value, but this particular morning it was off to the pet store—a real one in this case. Hand-in-hand Lila and Papa proceeded down the street until the pet store was plainly in sight. Lila, almost quivering with excitement, kept imagining Fluffy in her mind. He would be somewhat bigger than Miss Princess but not as, well, round as Mr. Trooper. *I am so polite*, she thought. Round is so much nicer than chunky or fat and she must always be polite to Mr. Trooper. Fluffy was then to be a black and white dog like Mr. Trooper but then it was the eyes that she focused on.

"Papa, do you remember the picture of Uncle Mark's other dog in his room on his boat?"

"Which one was that Lila? Do you mean the reddish and white dog? Her name was Aussie, I believe."

"Yes, yes, that dog! The one that was named Aussie and was also an Aussie, which really seems quite strange, Papa. Kind of like naming a girl, well, 'girl.'"

Papa smiled and said, "Yes, Lila. That particular dog lived with Uncle Mark for more than sixteen years and had a very special place in his heart."

"Well, Papa," Lila said thinking hard, "do you remember that Aussie had the brightest and bluest eyes that you had ever seen? They looked just like the sky on the sunniest of days in June, I thought. I want Mr. Fluffy to have eyes just like that, just the same, no different."

They were almost at the store now. Papa was thinking, Lila was thinking, and Papa and Lila's hands were held tightly and Papa was ready for almost any eventuality. Then, just the very moment they arrived at the store, from around the corner came a black and white Aussie with the bluest of eyes you had ever seen, and for the first time in her entire six-year-old life, Lila saw a dog smile. His teeth were blazing white and he was grinning from ear-to-ear.

Papa was looking at Lila, and seeing nothing, looked rather like a kick-boxer waiting for his opponent to do something of which he was not quite sure. Lila's giant eyes were so huge that they looked that they might pop right out of her head and end up on the sidewalk, which thankfully they did not.

Lila gasped for air because the dog was exactly what she had hoped for, what she had prayed for, what she had asked Santa Claus for in the secret letter that she had written even though Christmas was long past or was not quite here yet, she was not sure now. She was staring at the dog who was exactly, positively, the Aussie dog that she held firmly in her mind. Then the dog walked up, quite politely, and stuck out his paw and said something that astonished her right to the bottom of her small heart.

"Hello, Lila. I am Fluffy."

Chapter 4
Mr. Fluffy Settles In

Lila had never before seen a dog smile and certainly had never heard a dog talk, and yet on this day of days she had seen both.

"Papa, Papa! It is Fluffy! Oh my gosh, it is Fluffy, and right on schedule like I ordered him or something and he is smiling and he has introduced himself quite politely as you would expect."

Her father looked around, seeing nothing and hearing nothing, and then he looked around again just in case, and still not seeing anything, he smiled. It was one of those nice smiles, the sort of "anything you want Lila" kind of smiles that fathers often give their daughters because what else is to be done after all? Lila, however, was not looking at her father at all, not even a glance, as her eyes were totally focused on Fluffy and what might come next.

"Well, er, Fluffy. We are at the pet store, you know," said Lila.

"Yes, Lila," said Fluffy. "I can see that. This is where we arranged to meet, did we not? You were to be here and I was to be here and we are both here so it worked out just perfectly don't you think?"

"Gosh, I didn't think of it quite like that but you are right," Lila said. "So now that we have found each other, what are we to do? I have never owned a dog before, you know, and I am not sure what I am supposed to do or you are supposed to do exactly and, in any event, the dogs that I have met before never said anything but 'woof' when I asked them a question. So here you are and here I am and what is it we need to do next?"

"Well, we are at the pet store, you know, and I need a few things before we go home because just like you need dresses and purses and those pull back thingies that girls wear in their hair, I need a few things before we go," Fluffy said with a grin that did not retreat even one inch while speaking. Lila thought this was

pretty neat because it was a trick that she could not do herself.

"Yes, of course you need some things," Lila announced. "We shall get them for you right away," which was said at exactly the same moment as Lila was dragging her father into the pet store since this was the place, of course, where you got dogs the few things that are needed.

So Lila and Papa opened the door as Fluffy marched right in beside them so that the door did not close on his very furry tail and cause him to say "ouch." No, no "ouch" was needed, as they all headed into the store to start their walk down various aisles where all sorts of dog necessities and non-necessities resided. First was the invisible water bowl, and then there was the invisible food bowl, which took almost five minutes to pick out because some had flowers on them and some had bones on them and Lila suggested several but waited until Fluffy had decided. This was no quick process as dogs are always careful about these sorts of things, as they must deal with these bowls daily and it is a question of one's nose and how it fits in the bowl and that kind of thing which must be carefully decided. They stopped briefly to look at leashes but Fluffy indicated that none was necessary, and then there were the treats, only heart healthy of course, and dog food and what size kibbles and it was one half hour before Papa, Lila and Fluffy exited the store with the invisible dog supplies. Lila noted that they were paid for with invisible money and Lila thought that Papa liked that part of the shopping the best.

So the three of them set off back for home and Lila, as might be expected, could not wait to introduce Mr. Fluffy to Mama. Lila had decided that her new friend would just be Fluffy mostly, but for introductions and important stuff like that, then Mr. Fluffy would be more appropriate, and she was sure both Mama and Papa would agree with that. As they walked along she noted that the invisible dog supplies really didn't weigh much and carrying them was much more agreeable than going to the grocery store and having to carry all those heavy bags home. Though, she would have carried home whatever was necessary for Fluffy, of course.

Arriving at their apartment building, Fluffy smelled all around the front door. This was very important because one needed to find one's way home

regardless of what you were looking at, and the surest way to accomplish this task was by sniffing. Fluffy thought that it was a shame that people were not so good at this, but then people had other attributes he supposed, which might help them, though what they were he could not imagine. Then as they proceeded into the apartment building and passed the doorman, the situation was just a little funny as Lila was talking to Fluffy about this and that and the doorman looked at Papa with a quite inquisitive grin, noting that Lila was talking to no one. Papa smiled and made some remark like, "You know how six-year-olds are." Then they proceeded to the elevator where more sniffing was done just because that is what dogs do, and Fluffy, being a full-fledged Aussie, did it rather well, thank you very much.

Then the strangest of things happened, quite remarkable really. Upon Fluffy entering the apartment, the cats scattered in all directions and hissing could be heard from the living room to the kitchen. This is what cats do when aggravated you know, have hissing fits, and this is exactly what took place. Mama came rushing out of the kitchen and Lila's plan for a very polite introduction of Mr. Fluffy to Mama was pushed aside with the antics of the cats.

Papa just stood there, trying to make sense of it all. Why would the cats have a hissing fit when meeting an invisible dog that wasn't really there? It certainly seemed that the dog was there by the way the cats behaved, and Papa seemed quite confused about all of this. Fluffy jumped around and Mama made little noises seeming to indicate that she had no idea of what was going on or why it was taking place, whatever it was. Mama often behaved this way, which was no surprise to Lila, but the general confusion was not what she had hoped for when first getting home. She had imagined a polite little tea party and some nice conversation between her and Mama and Fluffy, but this did not seem to be the way things were going, so she just stood there until everyone calmed down.

Lila was not so good at just standing there, not her thing really, but she felt like under the circumstances this was the best idea, so that is exactly what she did. Generally Lila rose in the morning and scurried until bed time, and scurrying seemed quite natural and normal to her while quiet seemed just a waste of time. Lila, as typical of a six-year-old, had two buttons, on and off, and the space between them was very small indeed and quite hard to find with any precision. So there everyone stood. The hissing faded and one of

the cats poked one eye around the corner staring at nothing, except that was exactly the spot where Mr. Fluffy was standing which should surprise no one really.

Mr. Fluffy then said something, it was not English, Lila noted, and it was not exactly a bark or a woof either but a something, and the cat then poked more of himself around the corner along with his eye. Lila had noted that cats often slink. Slinking is something really that only cats can do and her cat slinked around this corner until its two eyes could be seen, very big eyes really for her cat. The cat stared at Fluffy, who seemed to wink in and out, which was quite unusual as he was already invisible, but there you have it. The cat then stopped and seemed to "harrumph," which is a cat kind of expression, and then turned her back the way a woman sometimes does to an unruly man, and walked off with its head held high as he had obviously decided to ignore Fluffy, ignore Lila and Papa, and ignore the whole situation entirely. The other cat had stopped hissing and had made his way to the sofa where he jumped up on it and proceeded to ignore anyone and everyone as well, so that Lila guessed that whatever had happened was now over and she could get on with the introduction of Mr. Fluffy to Mama.

"Mama, this is Mr. Fluffy," Lila said quietly and politely. "Mr. Fluffy, this is Mama." This she handled just the way she had been taught so that everyone had the correct introduction, which was very important for these kind of occasions.

Mama looked this way and that way and probably wasn't too sure exactly where she was supposed to look while Fluffy nodded agreeably and Papa blinked. It was now quite clear to Lila that neither Mama nor Papa could see Mr. Fluffy, though why this was she did not understand, but perhaps it had something to do with age and the difficulties that it brought to people as they got older. Yes, Lila decided, that must be it, and so from now on she would just have to point out where Fluffy was standing or sitting so that he did not get stepped on as Mama and Papa could not see him. There was something exciting about this really as she was the only one so far who could see Mr. Fluffy, and she grinned at herself in the way that young girls often do as if they hold some magic not shared with parents or other older people, and this they obviously do!

Chapter 5

Lila Discusses Taking Fluffy to School

"I do not want to go to school, Lila," Fluffy said with that certain grimace that often appears on a dog's face. "I have no interest in doing it at all, none whatsoever I tell you."

"But, Fluffy, I have told my friends all about you. Everyone is waiting to meet you. I have the nicest and bestest friends, and they are so excited to see you that I cannot even tell you how excited they are to meet you." Lila almost spit this out of her mouth like that awful tasting stuff Mama made her gargle in the morning which she just hated.

"Lila, that is the point," he reminded her. "I am an

invisible dog. Your friends can't see me and they will look at you very strangely when you introduce me and they don't think I am there. You can trust me on this. It will not go well."

Lila stood a moment and pondered this. She had assumed that all of her friends could see Fluffy because they were her age and not old people, and she had thought this was the trick of it, you had to be young to see an invisible dog, but now she was not so sure.

"You shouldn't have told them," said Fluffy gravely. "It should have been our secret and kept just between the two of us like a young girl and her best friend, and then it would not cause any problems. Now they are expecting to meet me and unless they are very, very special, they will not be able to see me."

So Lila stood there and Fluffy stood there and it was much too confusing for Lila because she had never considered this at all. So she stood and considered and considered some more, because this is what must be done with new problems. She wished that she had no problems, but life seemed to be full of them somehow.

"What am I to do now, then?" she asked Fluffy. "I

have already told everyone, just everyone, that you would be coming to school with me one day, and now what am I to do?"

Fluffy looked this way and that way and up and down and to this side and that side, as his giant blue eyes seemed to roll around in his head and no quick answer came to mind. "Lila, you are caught in a trap of your own making," he said, "and this is a two dog treat problem, I am sure. Could I please have one to start?"

"Yes, yes I will get you two treats right now because I have to go to school soon and we do not have much time, and if the answer takes two treats then let me get them both for you right now." She said this quite insistently as she walked into the kitchen where the invisible treat jar was, which is where the invisible treats were kept. She then returned with two invisible treats, looking similar to dog bones but made of something else entirely, and put them just so on the floor right in front of Fluffy.

Fluffy then settled down on his haunches, this is what dogs did when eyeing yummy treats as everyone knows, and he proceeded to gnaw on the first and closest treat to him. He found his paws quite useful at this time because he could hold the treat just so while he chewed upon it and rummaged about in his mind for some good answer. The first treat now being quite gone, he was working on the second, when it came to him. He knew it would be a two treat problem and he had just proved it, but he thought he would wait a moment longer to tell Lila, as using the proper words were very important with a young girl who might not know all of the words that he might have used otherwise.

Fluffy had often noticed that young girls only knew so many words or, if they knew more, they did not use them. He supposed that small mouths, which young girls had, might accommodate only small words, as they were easier to chew and then spit out which they did with rapid fire all during the day. Sometimes it was quite difficult to keep up with Lila's sentences and some words whizzed right past him before he could catch them, which made communicating difficult, though Lila did not seem to mind as she was used to this with her parents. Words were spoken, thrown right out of her mouth, and the problem was not with the speaking but with the listening, as words buzzed right past you if you were not careful.

So with the two treats being now finished as was the licking of his lips, always an important thing to do so as not to leave any crumbs behind, Fluffy turned his attention to Lila.

"Here is what we will do," he said. "I shall go to school with you and if some of your friends can't see me, quite likely as I have told you, then you will just have to tell them that I am a pretend dog, which is something like an invisible dog, but not exactly."

42

Chapter 6

Fluffy Goes to School

The bus arrived. The bus was not always on time, or even close to being on time, and as Lila waited with Mama she wondered just where was this silly bus. She supposed that some of the children were late which was why the bus was late, and she wondered if it was the strange ones or the normal ones or perhaps it was their parents as parents were sometimes late, she had noticed, especially the female parent. She was not quite sure why this was but Mamas were definitely more tardy than Papas. Perhaps this was because women run on a different time clock than men, and she wondered, when she was a grown up, if she was going to run on some different time clock. She hoped

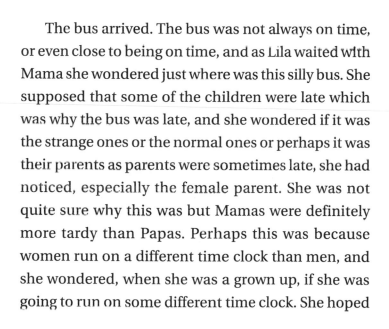

not because it was not generally polite to be late.

Her Papa had told her this more than once, and she even recalled that Papa had told Mama this, and it never seemed to make Mama all that happy when this was repeated to her. She always grimaced and gave at least fourteen reasons why she was late and Papa just nodded his head and grimaced back. He seemed to take very little note of all the excuses that Mama was offering, because even Lila at her young age thought they were excuses and not reasons, but she kept her mouth tightly shut. "No use entering that discussion," Lila said to herself. No reason at all.

Finding yourself caught between your Mama and your Papa when engaged in an argument, though more often small disagreements, was a place where you did not ever want to be, because it could result in that huge stare Mama was so capable of giving you or a very parental frown from Papa. No, better to keep one's mouth shut and look away and pretend that nothing at all was happening. This, in fact, was one more thing pretend was good for when you were a little girl.

So the bus doors opened and Lila got on the bus with Fluffy and they went almost all the way to the

back of the bus so they could find a comfy seat for both of them.

"Now, Lila," Fluffy said as they sat down. "Do not speak to me here, just smile and carry on as normal or all sorts of funny things might happen."

Lila looked around, it was apparent that none of the other children could see Fluffy or there would have been a big commotion about a dog being on the bus, and since there was none, it must be that Fluffy could not be seen. So Lila just stared out the window and hummed a little tune and pretended that this bus trip was like every other bus trip to school and things were just going on fine until one of her friends, Susie, came over to sit next to Lila and be friendly.

Just as Susie was about to sit down, right on top of Fluffy actually, Fluffy jumped into the aisle so this could be avoided. It was a close call. Lila was not exactly sure what happened if a person sat down squarely on an invisible dog, but neither did she much want to find out. So now Fluffy was in the aisle and Susie was sitting next to her speaking about something, though Lila was not paying attention, and then Susie said, "So what do you think, Lila?"

"Think, think about what? What did you ask? I am sorry to say that I was humming a little song and did not hear the question."

This was kind of true, almost true, as she had

been humming a little song but she had also been looking at Fluffy to make sure that he was okay and not stepped on by anyone. The last thing in the world that she wanted was her dog to get stepped on because she loved Fluffy, and no one who loves anyone wants them to get stepped on. Susie, in fact, had asked Lila how she liked Miss Bottomworth, their teacher, and having heard the question now, Lila said, "Fine, oh fine, she is quite nice I think."

Bottomworth was a strange name, Lila had to admit, a stranger name than most that she had heard but she had already figured out that Miss Bottomworth must have originally come from the strange girl category. She must have had strange parents, because no one, on purpose, would have picked the name Bottomworth if they had gotten to choose it. Lila did realize that Miss Bottomworth had not chosen her particular last name and that it had been given to her by her parents, so that it was rather like one of those heavy things that you had to drag through life, but then what could be done about those sorts of things? Nothing. She also knew that her teacher could get married someday and maybe one of the wedding presents would be a name change, something girls got to do if they wanted, or maybe that would be the main reason to get married, so that you did not have to lug Bottomworth along behind you all of the time. Lila had to admit, being truthful after all, that Bottomworth was a heavy lug.

She actually only knew of one other girl, she could care less what the silly boys had to drag around, that suffered the same fate as her teacher. This was one of her classmates, a French girl, whose real name was Melba du Pain which her friends had learned meant bread in French. "Pain" was bread in that language and so she had to lug around an unwanted nickname of "Melba Toast" which Melba hated, but she was quite stuck just like Miss Bottomworth.

Fortunately for Lila, she liked her name and her last name was not so bad either which was a blessing. Everyone seemed to be quite comfortable with Lila's name in fact and, at least, she would not have to marry one of those very yucky boys to get a name change, which was also a blessing. Not that she wanted to marry any one of them under any and all circumstances, though her mother had assured her that boys got better with age and wasn't Papa a boy after all? Papa was, of course, so perhaps Mama might, maybe, just possibly have a point. She would

see as she got older, but at six, she did not hold out much hope for it.

The bus had now arrived at school and she sat there quite politely until the other children had gotten off of the bus, so that she and Fluffy could make their way without Fluffy being trampled by one of her unknowing and unseeing friends. As she descended the steps in a very ladylike and polite fashion, with Fluffy right behind her, she noticed that he had bounded off the bus from the first step to the ground without using any of the other steps that were mandated for children to use to be safe, but then she knew that the same rules that applied to children did not necessarily apply to dogs. So she was okay with Fluffy's decision to bound instead of step. Then, as Lila trudged into the school building, it always seemed like a trudge after all when one went to school, she was approached by Trevor, one of the boys in her school who had decided, for some unknown and probably ridiculous reason, to say "Hello."

"Hello, Lila," he said, grinning like the overgrown baboon he was, or at least looked that way to Lila.

"Hello, Trevor," said Lila, looking away and up at the sky and in any direction at all so that she would not have to look at Trevor.

"How is your day, Lila, and have you heard the new Tootsie album that is out? It rocks."

"Trevor, I do not know who Tootsie is and if I did, I am sure that I would not like them at all because, well, because I am just sure I would not."

What she wanted to say, of course, was that if Trevor like them then she was quite positive, more than positive, that she would not like them, but that flew into the face of her mother's "always be polite rules," so she just took a deep breath and shook her head and continued her trudge into the school building. She did glance at Fluffy who was meandering along, a new word that she had just learned the meaning of, indicating that you are kind of sort of going but in no real hurry, which is exactly what Fluffy was doing. He was looking all around, sniffing the other children that could not see him and perhaps deciding if he wanted to be seen by anyone or not. Lila thought that Fluffy could do this, be seen or not, but she wasn't quite sure and he had volunteered nothing about this so it was only a guess on her part. Then as Lila wandered down the hallway to her classroom, she saw Miss Bottomworth. Her teacher was an African-

American woman with really curly hair and quite tall, so she was easy to pick out when walking or skipping down the hallway.

"Hello, hello, Lila and how are you this fine morning?" Miss Bottomworth inquired.

"Oh just fine, Miss Bottomworth, it is always a pleasure to come to school, you know," she said as she noticed that she did not see Fluffy at all, which was a good thing because Lila knew that dogs were not allowed in school and that Miss Bottomworth would be quite unhappy if she saw Fluffy. So she sighed a sigh of relief about this as Fluffy figured it out and laughed a sort of dog laugh, or perhaps an Aussie laugh, though Lila doubted if she could tell the difference. Miss Bottomworth droned on about the new classroom assignments and if Lila had understood her homework and said there would be reports made later or something, but Lila was watching Fluffy and not paying the kind of attention one should to teachers.

"What did you say, Miss Bottomworth? I am sorry that I missed it, I was distracted and whatever you said kind of flew over my head or past my ears without me catching it and I am quite sorry."

"It is okay, Lila, I know just how young girls are, easily distracted, as I was one once, you know." Lila found it hard to imagine Miss Bottomworth as a young girl, but supposed that she was some time in the very long ago past, which was way before her years of six. It hardly counted as anything past six years was so long ago that it may as well have been sixty years ago, and then her head began to hurt. She wondered if she had been infected by Mama's migraine, which she claimed to get from time-to-time. Whatever a migraine was she could not imagine, but something that resembled a headache which Lila had a few times before.

She did not think Miss Bottomworth was anywhere near sixty really, it was just that past some number everything might as well be sixty, and then it got quite confusing and so Lila dismissed it all like some complicated math problem that was not worth considering as the answer was of no use to her at all. There might be an answer, she knew that there was generally an answer, but what this answer was useful for was quite uncertain and certainly not for her normal life. She had often wondered why teachers and the like posed problems with no useful answers, and she had asked Papa about this once but only gotten a raising of the eyebrows which was Papa's way of saying that you were asking a dumb question, so she had stopped her inquiry and had not gone any further. Adults could be, well, so adult, but fine, if that was to be the way of it then she didn't need to know and was not going to ask again.

Then as Lila entered the classroom, she heard her friend Eleanor gasp. It was a big gasp, like a whooshing sort of gasp where one caught their breath and held onto it for fear of letting it out and spoiling something. All of her other friends were giggling about this and that, and the boys were making their usual grunting noises about nothing, but Eleanor stood there and her gasp was as big as her eyes and maybe twice as big. Now Lila had a lot of acquaintances at school and a handful of friends, but Eleanor was her closest friend. Of course, girls at six claim all of their friends are their bestest of friends, but Eleanor truly was her best friend and not just best friend but bestest, bestest, bestest friend. What Lila noticed right off was that Eleanor was not looking at her at all, not one bit, but was staring with great attention at Fluffy whom she obviously saw.

"Oh my gosh, oh my gosh, how did you get that

dog in here? How is he here and nobody sees him? Where did you get him? Why can I see him if nobody else can see him? Where did he come from? What is his name? He is so beautiful and so fluffy that I can hardly believe that he is a real dog!"

The rush of questions was just like snow falling down a mountain. Lila knew there was a word for this but it was long and complicated and she couldn't remember what it was. It felt as though Eleanor was asking questions just in this snow falling down a mountain way, and Lila was laughing being just delighted that Eleanor could see her invisible dog.

"Eleanor," Lila said, "you have it exactly, just exactly right that the dog is fluffy and because of that I have named him how you and I would both describe him, because we are the bestest of friends after all, and his name is Fluffy."

"Hello, Eleanor, I am Mr. Fluffy but you may call me just Fluffy seeing as you are Lila's closest friend," and with that, Eleanor fainted.

She fainted dead away and collapsed on the schoolroom floor, which caused Miss Bottomworth and all of the children to gather around Eleanor. The school nurse was called for and they all just

stood there not knowing what else to do. It was not common, quite uncommon in fact, for a child of six to just faint dead away, and no one had the slightest idea what to do except to call the nurse, which is what one did in these kinds of circumstances. Within moments the nurse came rushing in and gathered up Eleanor and took her back to the nurse's office.

"Children, children, please return to your seats. I am sure Eleanor will be quite alright. Probably something she ate this morning for breakfast that did not agree with her. Please be seated and I am sure that Eleanor will be back with us shortly."

Slowly, ever so slowly, the children headed to their desks, but there was a general murmur, a sound of many voices speaking at once, that indicated that everyone was not so sure Eleanor would be back shortly or if she was, that she might not be quite the same. Maybe even that she would not exactly be quite right as children did not faint without some reason, and of that the class seemed quite certain of really.

CHAPTER 7

ELEANOR RETURNS TO CLASS

They were just discussing history and George Washington being the father of the country and something about a "Pledge of all Injuns" which Lila thought was some Spanish song which was to be sung at all baseball and football games with "Jose, can you see," when Eleanor returned to class. Eleanor's last name was O'Connor and her family was from Ireland originally. Lila had once told Eleanor that she had very red hair, very red freckles and, just now, a very, very red face where all of her freckles had run together in one big splotch. In fact Lila had never seen Eleanor with a face quite this red and she thought that perhaps something just awful must have happened to her

in the nurse's office. Maybe she had to have a shot, and Lila just hated shots. They were one of the worst things in the entire world and Lila would go to any length, any, to avoid them. Mama had said that one shot avoided the flu but Lila was not going anywhere and she saw no reason to take this shot at all.

Eleanor had sat down by this time. She was paying no attention to the teacher at all, in fact she was doing nothing except staring at exactly the spot where Fluffy had sat down, and she was staring with great attention. Lila was trying ever so hard to pay attention to Miss Bottomworth but was not having such great luck doing it. Her eyes darted to Eleanor and then back to Fluffy and then she wondered why Eleanor could see Fluffy when none of the rest of her classmates could, obviously. She couldn't ask Fluffy about it now though, because while Fluffy was invisible and his voice could not be heard except by her and she supposed Eleanor now, she knew that her own voice was not invisible and could be heard, which just would not do sitting in the middle of class. Then she might get dragged off to the nurse's office for being crazy or something, and so she just had to sit there with her mouth shut.

As she sat there though, the girl behind her slipped her a note. She tucked it under her book because Miss Bottomworth frowned on passing notes and she did not want to get in trouble. Then just when her teacher turned and faced the blackboard to write something or another about George Washington and crossing some river, she took a quick peek at the note.

"I see a dog. It must be Fluffy. He looks just like you said he looked and he is the most beautiful dog I have ever seen outside of my own dog, Rex. He even might be more beautiful than him but one must be loyal to one's own dog, so they are in the same class I can say. How come you can see him and I can see him and no one else can see him? You must explain this to me. Then when Fluffy spoke to me in English and not in woofs or barks, I was just so surprised that I fell over I guess. I am fine now though, but you must talk to me immediately after class. You must."

Lila turned and looked at Eleanor and nodded and smiled which is just the sort of thing one does with their bestest friend in these kinds of circumstances.

Class ended and Lila headed to the playground before lunch. Eleanor was already there, waiting for her, jumping around like she could not wait one more minute for Lila, not even one more second.

"Tell me, tell me, tell me everything. I am about to burst and I don't understand any of this at all. How can Fluffy speak English and where did Fluffy come from and how did you find him and how did he find you and how long have you had him and what do your parents say and can they see him and talk to him and what about your cats and you must tell me everything whether you think it is important or not."

All of this flew out of Eleanor's mouth and it was so fast and so garbled that even Lila almost missed half of it because the words were jumping out as quickly, as any six-year-old girl can find them and then toss them into the air to be heard.

Lila started to explain, but then Fluffy himself walked up and said, "Perhaps I can explain. Eleanor, it takes a very, very special person to see me and speak with me. You have to be the most special kind of young lady because I am mostly invisible and cannot be seen or heard. There is a long explanation for all of this which doesn't really matter, but what does matter is that you and Lila are best friends and perhaps that has something to do with it."

Then Lila told her how she had met Fluffy and about the cats and her parents and how everything was going along just fine and all of the other details that should and must be shared with your closest friend. Eleanor's freckles had returned, they had been lost in a sea of a bright red face for a while, and Lila was glad to see that her friend was returning to normal. The girls had to go to lunch now and they asked if Fluffy was coming, but he declined and said that he was going to pick a nice warm spot on the playground to have just a little nap which is what dogs do at just about this time and Fluffy was no exception. So the girls promised they would stop back after lunch to gather him up, and off they went because young girls' tummies get hungry at just about this time and these girls were no exception. Fluffy was in his proper place and Lila and Eleanor were in their proper place and everything was just right with the world.

Chapter 8

Off to the Ice Cream Store

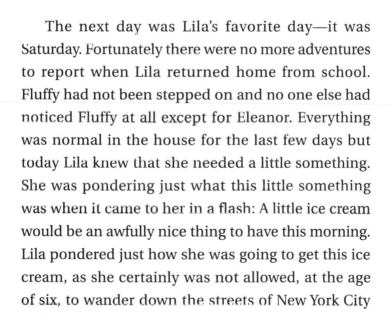

The next day was Lila's favorite day—it was Saturday. Fortunately there were no more adventures to report when Lila returned home from school. Fluffy had not been stepped on and no one else had noticed Fluffy at all except for Eleanor. Everything was normal in the house for the last few days but today Lila knew that she needed a little something. She was pondering just what this little something was when it came to her in a flash: A little ice cream would be an awfully nice thing to have this morning. Lila pondered just how she was going to get this ice cream, as she certainly was not allowed, at the age of six, to wander down the streets of New York City on her own. She knew that it was either going to have to be talking Mama into taking her or Papa into taking her or both, but she knew she could not do it by herself. Her parents were sitting at the kitchen table talking about something in which she had no interest, so she was not part of their discussion at all.

Sometimes parents could be very difficult and she was trying to imagine just how to discuss going to the ice cream store, because sometimes when she interrupted her parent's discussion she did not get what she wanted. Since she wanted some ice cream she had to come up with a plan to ease into this conversation without upsetting Mama and Papa. Lila then proceeded back to her bedroom. She thought it might be useful to discuss this with Fluffy.

Fluffy listened attentively, the good invisible dog that he was, and quietly pondered Lila's problem.

"Why don't you tell your parents that it is a lovely day, don't you think, and that we should all go out for a walk. Then while you are going down the street, you can just mention, just toss it out, that a little ice cream would be a wonderful thing this morning, don't you think?"

Lila thought that this was a perfect idea. So Lila

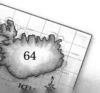

walked over to the kitchen table and followed Fluffy's advice exactly. Both Mama and Papa looked out the window and saw that Lila was right, it was a perfectly lovely day, and so they agreed.

Now it was winter in New York. A lovely day to be sure, but it was cold and so Mama bundled her up. Bundling was a long process that could take some time as it generally involved a shirt, then a sweater, then a big coat and finally some kind of scarf. These all must match of course, and fit together because Mama always told her that a properly dressed young lady must be appropriately attired, whatever that meant. This was also because, as Mama had so often told her, she didn't want her to get sick.

Sick was not good, she had been sick a few times and it was really no fun at all—quite the contrary, it was very unfun. Lila was not sure if "unfun" was really a word but, if not, it should be because that's what it really was. So as she bundled up, she found herself thinking that she must look very much like one of those teddy bears that she saw in the toy store windows. Bundling really meant growing fatter with all of these clothes and she did not wish to look fat, but then she supposed that it was probably better than being cold and then sick. So here she was, looking fat but feeling warm, and both Mama and Papa and her headed out onto the streets in that Saturday morning kind of way when wandering around was quite alright.

Now Lila was not sure where all of the stores were on her street or the ones close by. She knew some were here or there or someplace else, and her mind was rushing about in quite a whirlwind really, trying to place exactly where the ice cream store might be and then trying to figure just how to get Mama and Papa to start wandering in that direction. She looked over at Fluffy with that puzzled look and then he smiled, no words had been necessary, and he nodded off to the left and so she was quite sure that the ice cream store must be just exactly where he was pointing. She tugged at Papa and asked if they couldn't walk this way. This was just fine with Papa because he had no particular direction that he wanted to go, this not being a work day. So off the three of them went, in that going nowhere particular kind of way and then what do you suppose? There was the ice cream store exactly where Fluffy had indicated it might be found.

"Oh Papa, Papa! Look where we are, right in front of the ice cream store, and wouldn't it just be so nice

if we were to wander in to have a little something?" She often thought of a book that her mama read to her in one of these moments. It was called *Winnie the Pooh*, whatever a Pooh was, and she recalled that he was fond of a little something himself from time to time. Well, actually, it was most of the time, but then there was nothing wrong with that really as he was a bear, and bears, she had long ago decided, were fond of a little something most of the time.

This is why teddy bears also looked so, well, "bundled." She did not wish to think "fat" as she knew that was impolite, so that "bundled" must be the word. Maybe the book should have been called, "Winnie the Bundled" because at least she could have understood that. "Pooh" just did not mean anything to her except when that word was used to spit out something that tasted just awful, like spinach, but she did not think that the same meaning was useful here. "Winnie the Spit Out" could not be the right meaning of that book, in any event, because he was always eating a little something and not spitting it out but just eating more of it if he could.

In any event, the ice cream store was here, finally. It always seems to take so long to walk to them when you really want to get there, but here they were so they all went inside. Now Lila knew that life was full of choices and most could be easily chosen, but ice cream stores were such a dilemma. She had heard Mama use that word before and was pretty sure it meant that you had a number of choices, and she certainly did. She looked in that yummy bin and the next and the next one and if there was a dilemma she couldn't see it because they all looked, so, so good.

There was chocolate and strawberry and something called "Italian ices" which must have come from Rome or somewhere, but that was the only Italian city she could remember for the moment. Why they wanted to ship their ice all the way to New York, she had no idea, but there must be some reason. She had never seen ice that looked anything like theirs on Park Avenue or even 5th Avenue and she wondered just what kind of rain they must have to produce such ice, and she decided she must get Papa to take her there sometime. She was just going to say something about it when she realized that it could disrupt his quite good mood at the moment, so she decided to put off that discussion for another time. What she really wanted was some ice cream, and nothing was going to come between her and the ice cream. So she was looking and looking and considering carefully, when Mama said, "Lila, which one do you want, and do you want a cone or cup, or perhaps you want a sundae?"

Oh my gosh, oh my gosh! she thought. *I have been concentrating on one ice cream flavor or another and I have totally forgotten about sundaes. Yes, that is it, I must have a sundae of some flavor or another and then nuts, and whipped cream and then that really oh so good hot fudge sauce.* And then it dawned upon her that vanilla would just be the perfect choice. Sometimes things just came to you that way. In a big whoosh where you realized the most perfect choice all because you had thought of the question in a different way. Then she told Papa what she wanted, he ordered it, they got it and she sat down to the most delicious of afternoon pastimes, which is having a little something covered in hot fudge sauce. There were not many things in life better than that!

She and Mama and Papa then walked back to their apartment. She was not that fond of naps and remembered when Mama made her take them, but now, after that little something, she thought she might like to lie down just for a moment. Of course, she did not call it a nap which sounded so much like a word for a baby and not a big girl like her. She was almost grown after all. Fluffy was waiting for them all at home, as he had walked home early, and it always made her feel good thinking of going home to see Fluffy.

CHAPTER 9

IN SEARCH OF THE INVISIBLE PEOPLE

Today was Sunday. It was the day right after the hot fudge sundae day. It is hard to have a better day than that. It was funny how those two words sounded alike, Sunday and sundae, and didn't mean the same things at all. Lila wondered if there were other words like that. There must be, but none came to mind. Then it kind of leaked out from her thinking as she wondered just what she was going to do today since she did not have school, and so she concentrated on today, which did not have a corresponding todae. Though there might be some word which no one had taught her yet. Since there was no reason at all to consider this, however, she went on to think of an

adventure for today which would include Fluffy of course, as each adventure since he had arrived must include Fluffy, as he was now her invisible dog and so must be included.

Recently Lila had sat down with Fluffy and had a very confusing conversation with him about being invisible. One of the questions that she had asked was whether he was the only invisible dog or if there were others, and then if there were also invisible people. The smile that it had brought on his face was unmistakable like one of those very secret smiles when your math teacher asked if you knew the answer, and you did, and your face just lit up with knowing. It was very good to know things and even better to know things that other people did not. This was very different from guessing or hoping you knew the answer, or sometimes even praying that you knew the answer because no good would come from not knowing it.

Since Fluffy had explained it to her though, she now positively, absolutely knew the answer and that was yes, there are other invisible dogs and people. So, not having any particular plans for this Sunday, which she knew was not sundae, she wondered if she

might go and meet some of them and then how to do that.

What did you say to be polite and then how to get Papa or Mama to take her to meet them, became the subject of some very deep thoughts which caused her brow to furrow. Then her face scrunched up in that singular sort of manner that happens to six-year-old girls when they are trying to figure out something that is not so easy to figure out.

She thought and she thought and she thought some more, and nothing good was coming from these thoughts. It was not bad, just not good, and Lila felt rather like she was staring at a wall and trying to figure out how to get around it and that the wall was not helping but just standing there, being neither friendly or unfriendly, but not moving to any other place either. Walls could be oh so just that way as she had run into them before. So she plucked up her courage, took one final look at Fluffy, who was lying right in the sunlight on her floor and seemed in no mood to either move or talk but was just lying there half-awake kind of like dogs are prone to do, and she went off in search of Papa. She wanted to discuss going out to find other invisible dogs and people and to have a little Sunday adventure which is what Sundays were for.

"Papa, did you know there are other invisible dogs besides Fluffy and also invisible people?" Now Papa, who was deeply engrossed in reading the Sunday paper as was his tradition on Sunday morning, looked up from his paper with fairly good sized eyes and just looked at Lila. Whatever he might have been expecting to come his way on Sunday morning, this was not it, and so he just looked at Lila and tried to think where this was going. It was often difficult to figure out women, much less a six-year-old woman that was his daughter, and so he just stared at her, not being too sure where this conversation might lead.

Slowly, ever so slowly, he said, "No, Lila. I didn't know that," wondering just what might come next.

"Well, Papa, I spoke with Fluffy just the other day and that is what he told me, and since it is Sunday, with nothing particular to do, I thought we might go look for them and say hello."

Papa just sat there and pondered this. They had done museums recently and seen a movie about hobbits and other mystical beings, and they had done ice cream yesterday so that today did provide

an open space that could be used for something, but this had not been on his agenda, or even something that he had considered. On the other hand, some amusement could be found in this undertaking, so he just sat there and glanced up and down at his paper, and mused in that kind of far off way that Papas sometimes mused in. He, not knowing what to say, then pulled out his trump card, the one that all fathers everywhere use when in this situation: "Have you discussed this with your mother?" he asked.

"No, Papa. Mama is taking a bath and you know how she doesn't like to be disturbed when soaking. She always tells me this, as you probably know, and she is soaking now."

So, as anyone with children knows, Papa's trump had been overtrumped and the ball had bounced back into his court. This sort of thing is not so difficult with adults, but it is a very different game with children, especially his child. So his response must be framed with great care or some sort of tantrum, or worse, could be forthcoming.

So glancing this way and that and hoping that Mama might just at this moment emerge from soaking and provide some direction, he found himself cornered and did the thing that fathers often do which is to carefully accede to the wishes of their child. "So if Fluffy is right, Lila, where would we go about finding these invisible dogs and invisible people?" he asked.

A smile, a big smile, a giant fill-the-room kind of smile emerged on Lila's face. She had asked the same question of Fluffy and gotten an answer. So Lila was not only prepared, but in possession of knowledge that her father did not have, and that was just a wonderful thing.

Lila leaned on her right foot and then her left foot and did that little dance that children often do when in possession of such knowledge. There is no name for this dance. It is not the square dance or the waltz or one of those known dances that young ladies around the age of twelve are supposed to learn. This is an unnamed dance, danced only by four to eight year old young women when they know something that their parents do not, and so it is a very special dance that gets locked away in the hearts and minds of parents as their children grow older.

In fact, this is one of the things that is often sighed over by parents when their child reaches that age of

twelve or thirteen and becomes a teenager, because then this small dance is lost in memory, forever sheltered and protected by parents. As a teenager, everyone knows, a woman no longer does this dance because it just isn't done at her age. Ask any teenager, they will tell you this. This is also the age where "Mama and Papa" disappear to be replaced by "Mom and Dad" as the days of innocence end when something is lost but something is gained as one chapter shuts and another is opened. The Book of Life is a never ending story that is read in both a predictable and mysterious fashion.

"Fluffy is not so sure about the dogs, he has never seen another invisible dog actually, but the invisible people live in two places, Papa: the cornerstones of buildings and in the big rocks, the boulders of Central Park," said Lila in a great rush. Lila was relieved to get all of that out of her mouth. The dance slowed down and then stopped as she looked at Papa for his response. There was only one problem here, and that is that while she knew what big rocks were and she had been to Central Park many times, that she had no idea, none, of just what a cornerstone was or where they were to be found. This was a great mystery and when she had asked Fluffy about it, all she got was a smile, a very toothy smile.

Papa grimaced. His wide open eyes closed up and a look of great concentration was found on his face. "Where did Lila come up with that," was the clear expression on his face. This was followed by a second wind of "What am I supposed to do with it?"

Papa rubbed his bottom lip and looked at Lila, looked around for Mama to enter the room and then said, "Well, Lila, I have never seen any invisible people in Central Park, but then I never was really looking for them. Then these cornerstones, which cornerstones, in what buildings, and how do you approach these invisible people when you want to find them?" Just at that moment, just at that precise moment, Mama had entered the room, being done with her soaking, and she had a very mischievous twinkle in her eye.

She said, "Well, you knock on the cornerstone of course, and just say 'hello', as anyone who knows anything knows." Papa had that "oh boy here we go" look on his face now and he knew that Mama had poked him right in that one spot in his ribs where his wife tended to poke when prodding him to do something or another, but he supposed he could go along with all of this. Today was Sunday, after all, and

just the right day for these kind of adventures, when museums and movies could be set aside.

So there was all of the normal parental conversation and the usual teddy bear bundling in wintertime, and it had been decided that off they go in search of whatever creatures might be found that were invisible and found living in cornerstones and boulders. So off they went, down to the subway, to head down to Wall Street to inspect cornerstones, the place where most of them could be found according to Papa. What did they find as they sat down on the subway? Fluffy was already there waiting for them. How he performed this trick was something beyond Lila, but being invisible it seemed just likely enough and so Lila didn't ask him, and besides, it would have been awkward to ask him sitting in the subway with all kinds of strangers hanging about. Lila preferred to be thought of as a normal girl and talking with someone who no one else could see would involve either explanations or strange stares, and so she just sat there. She stared at her shoes and said nothing while squeezing Mama's hand, which is what young ladies do when riding in the subway.

Upon arriving at Wall Street, they trudged up the

stairs and out into a rather forceful blast of cold air. Lila was not all that fond of cold air, or of winter for that matter, and her thoughts turned to Princess and Mr. Trooper and being on Uncle Mark's boat as a way to cheer herself up, but it only helped some. Actually, not so much, because the harshness of the cold air was a great distraction from trying to think pleasant thoughts. Your face felt numb and your hands felt numb and your brain was not far behind, in Lila's considered opinion. "Numb, numb, numb," she said to Mama when asked how she was doing and Mama only nodded in understanding.

So here they were, and some famous cemetery or another was just across the street Papa told her. Now why a place for dead people was famous was so far beyond her at the moment, and so past anything that she cared about, that she didn't even inquire. At the moment she cared about her hands and her feet and her toes and her nose and that was it. They were all freezing and complaining loudly in her mind, and she wondered if her thought up adventure was such a good idea after all. Yet they kept going, all holding hands, all with bowed heads in the wind as they looked for their first cornerstone.

So they were all standing there, and it was a really old building, Lila imagined, and Papa was peering at the corner block trying to read the words. This must be what a cornerstone is, which is the corner block of stone of some old and musty building, and why the invisible people or dogs or whatever would want to live in one of these was far beyond her imagination. Then the three of them joined hands again and slipped and slided on the ice as they made their way around the bottom of the building while Papa was obviously looking for something or another, but it was too cold for him to say what and also too cold for Lila to ask what.

So they just kept going around one edge of the building and on to the next, until Papa found what he was looking for, which he pointed at and said, "Cornerstone." Not much else could be heard in the whoosh of the freezing wind. So they stood there and Lila looked at Fluffy, who was just standing there like it was some day in June and not affected at all by the cold. Fluffy was gazing ever so thoughtfully at the cornerstone as Papa inquired just what they were supposed to do next.

"Fluffy, here is the cornerstone. Now what are

we supposed to do?" asked Lila quite politely. Fluffy walked over to the cornerstone and peered intently at it and then sat down on his haunches in what appeared to be a number over sixty kind of problem, and said nothing. Papa was looking at Lila, and Mama was looking at Lila, and Lila was looking at Fluffy wondering just what was supposed to be done now. The screaming wind had died down at the backside of the building, and yet it was still numbingly cold as they all stood there and waited, not sure exactly what for.

Then Fluffy got up and walked directly over to the cornerstone and scratched it with his paw. It was kind of like a polite knock, but then she wasn't exactly sure as dogs tend not to knock when entering rooms. She had never seen a dog knock, real dog or imaginary dog, and so she wasn't sure if this was knocking or scratching, which is something dogs did do sometimes especially while on comfy couches or on the floor just before they settled in. So they stood there waiting, even Fluffy seemed to be waiting, and then Fluffy announced, "They aren't home," and sat down again.

"Papa," said Lila. "They aren't home." Papa just

nodded and did that grimacing thing once again
while Mama inquired if they would be home anytime
soon. Fluffy just shrugged his shoulders, which are

really haunches but that was of no importance at the moment, and it appeared as if it was an unanswered question. Lila thought that it was easy enough to figure out if people, invisible or not, were home, but much more difficult to figure out when they would be back exactly. This wasn't like some shop with a sign in the window that said, "Lunch, back at 12:30" which was something done by shops but not generally done by homes, and so they could be out for a snack, or in Iceland for all they knew, and the lack of an answer hung over them all.

CHAPTER 10
THE SEARCH CONTINUES

Since no one seemed to respond to Fluffy's knock, or perhaps, to be more accurate, scratching, the three of them trundled off, but to where Lila was not quite sure. At first she thought they were going to head back to the subway to head home, but then Papa seemed to think better of it or different of it in any event, and they walked over to another building to inspect it. This one was even older and mustier than the last one, and appeared to Lila as if had been there just forever. Now Lila knew that "forever" was a very long time, she wasn't exactly sure just how long forever was, but a very long time was something she thought she had right.

Lila looked at the building and wondered if it had been built by the Pilgrims, the founders of the country that she had learned about in school, but she wasn't exactly sure if they knew how to make big buildings such as this one. They might have, she just didn't know. She thought briefly of asking Papa about this, but when she opened her mouth, it was so cold that she thought her tongue might get stuck to the roof of her mouth and so she clamped it shut in a hurry. The answer was far less important than the well-being of her tongue and so she didn't ask from the question.

Papa was now examining the writing on the edge of this building like the other one, and then they started off again around the corner until they reached the opposite side. Another examination took place and then Papa pointed again at the block of stone and announced, "Cornerstone," in a very commanding voice while Mama nodded and Fluffy came over for an inspection. Then Fluffy began the polite knocking/scratching yet again. It was quiet, very quiet as they all strained their ears for some sort of noise, and then Fluffy did the oddest of things: He began to dance.

It wasn't the dance of just before Fluffy took care of his business, that she had seen often enough, nor was it the dance that was reserved for the postman when he showed up, which wasn't really a dance but more like a warning that people in funny gray uniforms were not so welcome at their apartment, but it was a circling kind of joyous dance really like when one stumbles upon old friends in a quite unexpected place. People, she had noticed, also did this dance when coming upon a neighbor in an art gallery or some department store. Lila was eyeing Fluffy and her parents were eyeing her, and she caught her breath and waited for what might come next.

Now most moments in life run on in a very connected sort of way. They are kind of like a paved road where one stone leads to the other and you really never think about it unless you are pondering the various mysteries of life, but then there are those occasional moments where things go haywire and become very disconnected, and this was certainly one of those moments. The last moment did not lead to the next moment at all, and her eyes, while always so, so big, became so much bigger as a blond head of mopped hair ever so slowly pushed open the stone which turned into a larger door and said very politely, "Hello."

Lila looked at Mama and Papa and it seemed

as if every part of their body was shuddering with either excitement or apprehension—she couldn't be sure which.

"May I help you?" said the fuzzy blond head of a young girl about Lila's age. Lila thought Papa might drop to his knees in surprise, while Mama began to shake and stammer about nothing as she dropped Lila's hand and left it dangling. Fluffy then said something or barked something and the young girl said, "Sure, come on in."

The door was very strange. It was just inches above her own small head when she walked in. Then the same inches above Mama's quite higher head when she entered, and the same inches above Papa's much taller head when he walked through the doorway. How this worked Lila had no idea, but the three of them stepped into the cutest house which looked like it belonged to small blue fairies or some very cute elves in one of her fairytale books. She glanced at her parents and they were both quivering and she was afraid that Mama and Papa might come undone as they entered the room.

There was a funny wooden table in the hallway and Papa seemed to be holding onto it for dear life. Lila thought that Papa and Mama were breathing hard before, because of the cold she was quite sure, but now they were gasping for breath as if confronted with something they neither understood nor believed in and silence gripped them all in a deafening kind of way. When a moment is dead quiet and aloud with a huge roar at the same time, it is a different kind of moment and that is exactly what they were all experiencing—a very different kind of moment.

"Who is it?" boomed from the other room.

The mopped blond head sitting on top of a very cute and childlike female body said, "Fluffy and his friends."

Now Mama and Papa had mostly humored Lila. When Lila spoke with Fluffy or announced that it was time for a treat, they generally smiled at each other and nodded in that parent kind of way when children play pretend. There would be plenty of time later in life for unpretend, and so these were the special moments of childhood. This is what most parents think and this is how it goes in every country on Earth.

However, now Lila's parents were confronted with something else entirely, and the rubbing of eyes, which seems to take place in moments such as these, did not dispel what was right in front of their noses. Here they were in a house inside of a cornerstone in the middle of downtown Manhattan. The house was here, inside a cornerstone, which shouldn't be here at all, couldn't be here at all, not at all.

"Well show them in, Heidi," said the very big voice. "Just don't leave them standing in the hallway."

Heidi, obviously her name, said, "Oh yes, Papa. They are just catching their breath."

Fluffy was dashing about sniffing everything,

Lila was just staring wide-eyed at Heidi, and Mama and Papa continued to gasp for breath as if Elijah the prophet had just shown up for dinner and sat down. Events had turned in a very uncertain and unbalanced way, and Lila's parents, often prepared for any eventuality, had now found one for which they were neither ready nor prepared. A certain air of unease had entered the room.

Lila had seen the "air of unease" enter the room before, but never one that smelled this strongly as she just waited for her parents to catch their breath. Finally, after a very long time, Papa stumbled forward and into the next room where a reddish bearded, rather round fellow was sitting in the biggest armchair Lila had ever seen, and was smoking a pipe. This amazed Lila on many levels. First, Mama did not allow smoking in the house, and then the size of his beard was the biggest she had ever seen and finally they were in a house inside a cornerstone and that both Mama and Papa could see everything just as well as she could. "Startled" was too small of a word and she was not exactly sure what the word should be but it must be a giant one to describe this occurrence.

"Well sit down," said Ragnar which was his name

as they all would learn shortly. So Lila sat down on the stoop in front of the fireplace, and Papa sat down, really kind of thumped down and not sat down, in another large armchair, and Mama also sat down in a very pretty blue frilly chair where she did not sit down really either but kind of perched like a frightened bird as if some predator might swoop down at a moment's notice.

"My name is Ragnar," he said as if this sort of name was the most normal in the world, which it was not for Lila and her parents. Lila assumed that Ragnar was Heidi's father, but made no mention of anything quite yet as she knew that Papa must take the lead now as things were so uncertain that being an adult was now in play and so she waited. It was a long moment and good expanse of time before Papa cleared his throat.

He said, "I do not believe I am here, I do not understand how we are here and I do not even know where here is but if you could explain it to me I would be appreciative."

The laugh was big, it filled every space in the room, there was no small amount of air that was not filled with the laugh and it seemed to shake the very rocks on the stoop where Lila now sat. Lila had only heard this kind of laugh once before and that was the "Ho, Ho, Ho" laugh from Santa Claus once and she thought that this laugh was even bigger and grander than that one. The twinkle in Ragnar's eyes brightened up the room considerably, Lila noticed, and the gasping for air by her parents commenced again as the laugh began while they both waited for an answer.

"Many years ago, many, many years ago," said Ragnar, "a group of us left Iceland because it was so awfully cold that our breath practically turned into icicles. So we got into our longboats and sailed south. We had hoped to find the palm trees and sandy beaches we had heard rumors about, but we ran into what you now call New York and, it being considerably warmer than Iceland, we stayed. At first we lived in boulders and other large rocks, which is our tradition, but then we found the people in the city amusing, so some of us moved into the cornerstones of your buildings so that we could watch you more often and grin at the way you behave. Actually, this is the first time in many years that I have allowed someone to see me or my family, but then no one else has showed up with Fluffy or his relatives either, in

all of this time, so I made my decision and had Heidi bring you in and here you are."

Papa stared at the fireplace, at the cobblestones on the floor, at the rafters in the ceiling, at anything and everything except Ragnar and then quietly said, "Oh, I see," which he obviously did not, but then what was one supposed to say?

Mama looked at Papa, just stared at Papa as if he would suddenly make everything alright and normal again. When this did not take place, her glance shifted to Lila just to make sure she was actually there and safe. It is quite important to mothers, as we all know, that their children are there and safe, and Lila's mother was no different than the rest in this aspect of life. So Papa saw but did not see at all and just sat there. He was somewhat afraid that if he said too much that everything might disappear and he would find himself in some hospital. That he had fallen down in the street, and when this did not happen, it slowly dawned upon him that he was actually here after all and not lying in some hospital bed after being awakened from some type of dream.

"Ragnar," Papa said, "it is very difficult for me to believe that I am actually here, so if I seem somewhat

surprised and startled, will you forgive me?"

The laughing face turned into a knowing smile and Ragnar said, "Yes, bumping into new things is always somewhat surprising as you are never quite sure what the surprise might be or mean. I shall start out with the fact that you are actually here, quite safe, and that I let you in out of respect for Fluffy, who obviously brought you here for some reason. I am unsure of the reason I must say and Fluffy has not shared the secret with me yet, but he must have some reason, of that I am quite sure."

Just then Ragnar winked out of existence and then back into existence as if to show Papa exactly what he could do if he so chose, and the gasping for breath started once again. "How do you do that?" asked Papa. "Exactly how is that done?"

Ragnar just smiled, a very nice and kindly sort of smile, and said that there were some things in the universe that could not be so easily explained. He said that this was one of them and that Papa would have to wait awhile for the explanation, as this kind of knowledge could cause all kinds of havoc for his people and even Papa's people because of what could be done with it. Papa nodded, just sat there and

nodded, and waited for Ragnar to continue.

"Our people are quite old. We age slowly, very slowly, you would be surprised with the age of Heidi in your years, and yet she is the equivalent age of your daughter, perhaps not in years but certainly in maturity. Heidi is a young, dashing around, full of life at every moment kind of girl just as, what is her name, your child?"

"Lila," Papa said while Mama nodded her head, as if this was a significant moment in which the name of her daughter was revealed.

"Ah yes, Lila," Ragnar said. "A nice name. A solid kind of female name with a touch of elegance. It fits her exactly. Names are like that, you know. They should be chosen carefully for the wearer carries them around for all of their lives and a name, itself, can define the person that wears it."

Just then an older female burst into the room. "Now what is going on, and who are our guests?" and then it dawned upon the woman, who must surely be Heidi's mother by her looks, that she not only had guests but human guests, which is not what she was expecting at all.

The gasping for breath began once again. It was

not from Mama or Papa this time but centered on the woman of the house, of that there was no doubt, given how she had stormed into the room. She just stood there and surveyed each of them, like mothers of all types do, and then announced, "Oh hello, well hello, I am Kristin."

She then looked at Ragnar, quite hard and seriously at Ragnar, and inquired demurely, somewhat sweetly, as to exactly what was going on. Most mothers, and Kristin with certainty, did not like surprises found in their living room that they were not expecting. It was quite obvious that Mama, Papa and Heidi's mother had all bumped into a day with a very big surprise inside of it, and it was natural enough to ask anyone, everyone, just exactly what was going on. The question was certainly going to be answered by her husband; of that much she was sure. She would get an answer.

Ragnar fiddled and Fluffy fiddled, but no one took notice as all eyes were on Ragnar, waiting for some sort of explanation.

"Fluffy brought them. He is obviously an invisible dog and he must have had some reason for bringing them around, so I let them in."

97

Kristin nodded, blinked, and with furrowed brow said, "Well, you might have checked with me first, but it is obviously too late for that. Now we shall see what needs to be done."

Fluffy sat there, Lila sat there, Mama and Papa sat there because there was nothing else they could do as they weren't entirely sure they were really, actually, sitting there anyway. Kristin, hands on her hips and looking quite in charge, was looking this way and that way with a furrow in her brow that looked very much how she looked when Heidi misbehaved and had to be dealt with in some adult manner where a lesson needed to be taught. Humans in her house, what next? This question was pretty much etched on Kristin's face, and the deciding was hanging in the air.

Now there was no law or regulation that the invisible people couldn't be seen if they so chose. Neither was there any document that forbids inviting humans into your house, so it wasn't the kind of thing when you were in violation of some long ago worked out code. It just wasn't done, though.

Kristin could not remember when a human had been invited into the house of one of her people and it was certainly the first time that there had been a

human inside her house or even her parents' house, and of that much she was certain. So she just stood there, hand planted firmly on her hips in the way that mothers, invisible or not, do when confronted with uncertainty and when something must be done. *Well, there is nothing else to do about it,* thought Kristin and so she did what polite women do everywhere when in this situation. Turning to Mama, Kristin smiled and said, "Can I get you some coffee or tea or something? I have some quite nice tea that I just bought at the grocers and I think you would enjoy it." Lila's mother was the one who blinked now and nodded. Off Kristin went to the kitchen to prepare a little something for her guests.

The good tea service was brought out. This was not a day or an occasion for the normal everyday tea platter. Tea was passed around and yet a very awkward silence hung over the room. Papa was not sure what he should say or even could say without seeming to be impolite. Mama just kept blinking, and Lila and Fluffy had both realized that this was not the time to say anything at all as this was some kind of grown-up moment and it would have to be sorted out by those that were grown-ups already.

Ragnar, shuffling about in his oversized chair, finally broke the silence by announcing, "I just can't tell you." Which seemed to answer the questions that were sliding around in the room without anyone asking them. Papa smiled and seemed relieved to have an answer for many of the things that he was about to ask, and the tension eased slightly for everyone.

"We must all think on this," Ragnar offered. "And we must all proceed with some care as there is a very delicate balance here which must be respected. To be quite honest, I am not sure exactly what is to be done now and I need some guidance from the Council of Elders which is the group that I must consult with to know exactly what to do next. To be quite open, I am feeling a little lost now, well, quite a bit lost now," he admitted. "I don't want to do the wrong thing and find my friends staring at me and nodding in that disapproving sort of way when I see them. You must understand, there are the New York Council of Elders and the Iceland Council of Elders. I am not even sure how far up this will have to go as new territory has been entered here and the consequences must be considered carefully." Ragnar then looked very carefully and very directly at Fluffy and said, "And you, sir. What were you thinking? Just what were you thinking when you brought our guests here today? That is what I would like to know."

Fluffy's tail moved to the left and then to the right, and a slight swooshing sound could be heard upon the floor as if one were cleaning up a few crumbs from breakfast. Fluffy then smiled. He just smiled and his rather large blue eyes became very bright and then he stretched, that very long dog stretch when front paws go forward and back paws go backward, and a dog's body is elongated past what people are expecting. He said nothing however, not one word in his language or any of theirs, and a very mischievous kind of smile was all that was forthcoming. He then moved towards the door as if it was time to go, and Ragnar looked on with a very puzzled expression but said nothing as he realized that, for whatever reason, no answer would be coming, and so he scratched his head and looked at his wife.

Just then, Papa stood up and said, "Well, it is probably time to go. Lila has school tomorrow and it will be getting dark soon and it is a long way back up town." Kristin was nodding so Heidi started nodding and then everyone was nodding because no one

ICELAND

knew quite what to do and so this was as good a way to end their first meeting as anyone could obviously think of. Mama and Lila and then Papa shuffled towards the door.

"We will be in touch," said Ragnar. "Thanks for coming and have a pleasant evening. It is probably better not to discuss this with your friends at this point. No sense in stirring up a lot of troubles when none needs to be. If I can just ask you to wait and see what we are to do now, I would appreciate it. I mean, I am not telling you what to do or anything but I think this would be the best course for the moment and so that is my advice."

Papa smiled and said, "I can assure you that my wife and I will not be discussing this with anyone. First, no one would believe us, and then everyone would think we had wandered past the outskirts and so nothing, I assure you, will be said. I must tell you that I am not even honestly sure that this all happened. I mean, I am here, and I have pinched myself several times and this all seems to have happened and is happening, but then part of me is not so sure. When we agreed to take on an invisible dog I was fine, but I had no idea that it would lead here and so not only

must you think about this, but so shall I. Thanks for a pleasant afternoon. It was great to meet you all and have a wonderful evening."

With that there was more nodding and Papa grabbed Mama's hand and they headed towards the very curious door that adjusted to everyone's height as if by magic which, Papa thought, might be exactly what it was. Lila scurried along and Fluffy followed them all as if to make sure that they all got out without a worry. The doorway went up and down with each of their heads and then they were back in the cold and thankful that they were all bundled, and when they turned back to wave goodbye, no one was there.

There was just the very old building, the cornerstone with the words written on it and the silence of a freezing winter's day in New York. It was like nothing had ever happened and yet it had, and there was nothing to be done about it now except to accept what had happened and get on with it. Each of them was quiet as they headed back toward the subway and each of them was lost in their own thoughts. Except for Fluffy who smiled, Lila noticed, as if he knew exactly what had happened and exactly where they were all going. This made Lila a little more nervous the more she thought about it.

CHAPTER 11
AND WHAT NEXT

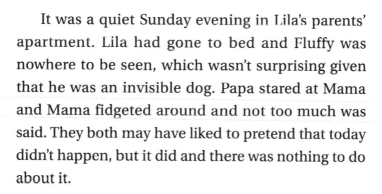

It was a quiet Sunday evening in Lila's parents' apartment. Lila had gone to bed and Fluffy was nowhere to be seen, which wasn't surprising given that he was an invisible dog. Papa stared at Mama and Mama fidgeted around and not too much was said. They both may have liked to pretend that today didn't happen, but it did and there was nothing to do about it.

"It wasn't what had taken place that took place," Papa had said earlier, "but what to do about it that mattered now." They wouldn't discuss it with anyone, that was for sure. No one would accept it and no one would believe it and nothing good could come from bringing it up. It would remain a family secret for the present, but what might come of it all was hard to tell.

Papa and Mama had almost no information about this Council of Elders, either the New York one or the Iceland one. What they might decide was anyone's guess and when they might be contacted about it was also a great unknown, if they were ever going to be contacted at all. They just had to wait, and waiting was not that easy whether you were six or much older, and that was one of the things about life that didn't seem to change regardless of your age. Waiting wasn't all that much fun but there was nothing to be done about it, so waiting is what all three of them would have to do. The culprit in all of this was definitely Fluffy, but what was on his mind or what is intention might be was also an imponderable and he wasn't saying anything. It was funny in a way. Normal dogs couldn't talk and this one could, and yet he wasn't and so they were no better off in the end.

Papa had asked Lila on the way home in the subway if Fluffy had said anything else to her, but she only shook her head "no."

"There is more here than meets the eye," Papa said to Mama. Mama winced and said, "That was a terrible

pun." Which was not what Papa had intended, but she was right. It is funny how certain thoughts creep into your mind and manage everything and that was one of those thoughts that had accomplished its task. Somehow the normal problems of life seemed less important at the moment, work seemed totally unimportant and what had mattered yesterday had been replaced with invisible people, invisible dogs, Councils of Elders and Lila's father could not even imagine what might come next. One day you are leading a perfectly normal life, and then something happens and the whole thing gets tossed up in the air like leaves on a winter's day, and who knew how or where they all might land.

The days passed by, calmly enough given the circumstances, and no one said too much about what had occurred. One thing that was certain was that there had been no discussion about what had taken place with anyone. The three of them, well four of them if you counted Fluffy, had discussed it, but that was as far as it went. Fluffy, however, wasn't saying much and about all that he added to any conversation was a smile and a nod and sometimes a wagging tail, as dogs do this with some frequency just because they are dogs, you know. Papa had tried to speculate on what would happen next, but since he had no idea or even the faintest glimmer, he gave up on this task after a few days and decided that waiting was not only the best avenue but it was the only avenue, really.

Mama puttered about in the kitchen and made sure that Lila did her homework and did all those motherly things that mothers do, because just as Fluffy often engaged in tail wagging, Lila's mama was the mother and did what she was supposed to do because there was no other way of it. Lila observed all of this in a very polite sort of way which is exactly what she had been taught. Young ladies thought about the goings on in their homes, of course, and Lila had been trained by Mama to be a lady and not just a young girl.

Lila watched Papa fret, but quietly, as he tried to understand it all and he looked pretty much like she did trying to figure out a math problem which this whole thing was, in a funny sort of a way. Lila also watched her mother as she puttered. Lila had known for some time that Mama puttered and she supposed it had something to do with keeping busy and "setting a good example," which was a subject that

Mama remarked upon often enough. She had heard Mama say this to Papa on many occasions, "We have to set a good example," and since they always both agreed upon this, that is what they did, or at least Lila thought that was what they did, but then she had so few examples to compare it to and she supposed that all of her friends must have parents setting their own good examples so this was just the way of normal life at six.

Sometimes Lila wondered if this was the normal way of life at seven, but she had not gotten there yet and she supposed that she would find out. It was difficult to know if seven was different than six, but then five had come and gone and turned into six which was pretty much the same except that she had grown and gotten new clothes and changed teachers at school, but the rest was pretty much the same. Growing, she noticed, was a children sort of thing, as Mama and Papa did not get any taller or need new clothes, though Mama said she did from time to time. Lila however, had already figured out that this was not because of growing. Mama once explained to Lila that women required new clothes because of fashion, but fashion was like an over sixty math problem and not easily understood. It had something to do with the change of seasons and what other women were wearing and "keeping up," but then Lila's mind started to hurt when all of this was considered and so she just put it aside and left it to Mama.

Fluffy, and her various dolls, and homework, and the problems of her friends at school, and all of this was quite enough, Lila decided, to keep her busy during the day. Lila had noticed that when the discussion of fashion had come up between Mama and Papa, Papa rolled his eyes, but then this was something that Papa did with regularity. Lila decided it was a Papa kind of thing, him being a male, and that discussions of fashion or boxes arriving from department stores were two subjects that caused Papa to wiggle his eyes around like wheels on a car. Some box arrived, the eyes turned and discussions about money took place. Lila learned long ago that when boxes arrived, the safest place was in her own room and so that is where she retreated.

Whatever fashion was, Lila decided that it brought along with it all kinds of other problems, and so she was not taken too much with fashion even though Mama said it was part of a young lady's life. Lila was fine being bundled in the winter and less bundled in

the summer and in-between, one made progress in one direction or the other depending upon if it was spring or fall. That was enough fashion for Lila!

CHAPTER 12

NEXT ARRIVES

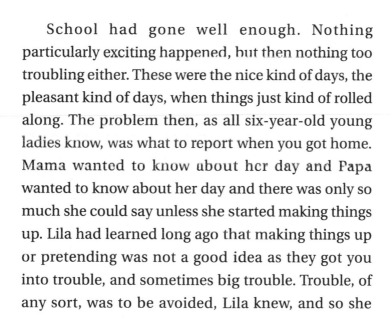

School had gone well enough. Nothing particularly exciting happened, but then nothing too troubling either. These were the nice kind of days, the pleasant kind of days, when things just kind of rolled along. The problem then, as all six-year-old young ladies know, was what to report when you got home. Mama wanted to know about her day and Papa wanted to know about her day and there was only so much she could say unless she started making things up. Lila had learned long ago that making things up or pretending was not a good idea as they got you into trouble, and sometimes big trouble. Trouble, of any sort, was to be avoided, Lila knew, and so she just smiled in her very cute kind of six-year-old way and reported on what had taken place and left it at that, as she knew perfectly well where things should be left, right at that, and nothing more. So they were all sitting there at the kitchen table and Lila had reported, and then the doorbell rang.

You must understand how unusual this is in New York City, when the doorbell rings and you are not expecting company. Lila and her family were a civilized sort and they had a doorman that announced when people came calling and the doorman had said nothing of it. No phone call had been made announcing, "so and so is here," and all of a sudden their doorbell rang and everyone's eyes were wide open with expectation. It could be a neighbor, it must be a neighbor needing some sugar or vanilla extract or some ingredient they needed to cook dinner and were out of or couldn't find in their pantry. It may just be that it was so cold outside that some neighbor had come asking for this or that so they didn't have to get all bundled themselves and trudge down to the grocery store. This is what Papa was thinking and announced as he made his way towards the front door, "Must be some neighbor."

Papa then opened the door as Lila and Mama looked on, but strangely enough, oddly enough, no one was there. Papa looked this way then that way down the hall and was just about to close the door, when a voice said, "Are you alone and can I come in?"

The whooshing began. Papa whooshed and Mama whooshed and Lila whooshed all at once and it was the only other sound in the room. The last time Lila had heard whooshing like that was in Ragnar's house and here it was again, and still no person could be seen at the front door. Fluffy then bounded out from the kitchen where he had been sitting, and now the sounds were whooshing, tail swishing and a funny creaking as if someone or another was rocking back and forth on his feet.

"Yes, yes, come right in," said Papa in a very small voice, and Lila peered intently at the front door wondering just who might be arriving.

"I am Halfur," said the voice, "and the Council of Elders has asked me to stop by and have a word with you." Lila noticed Fluffy nodding and more tail wagging so she wasn't afraid, though she might have been in other circumstances. Then the most curious kind of large, round, elf kind of person, popped into

the room. He looked kind of like Santa Claus, but not quite, and he was the most out-of-some-story-book kind of person that Lila had ever seen and she wondered just which kind of story he had popped out of to make his appearance.

He was certainly not tall but he was definitely round. That was the first thing she noticed. It wasn't the clothes really, but he was bundled in his own sort of way, meaning that he was a bundled person naturally. Lila would not use the word "fat," she knew this was impolite, so "bundled" it was, which was just the way that God had made him, she supposed. He also had a large red beard, like Ragnar's, so she supposed that the invisible males favored red hair which came as no surprise as the invisible people seemed mostly like her and her family, but then also not at all.

Halfur was also stretching up and down like he had something important to say, but then it had not come out quite yet and so while it was waiting to be evicted from his mouth it just sort of bounded up and down between his forehead and his toes. It was a curious kind of moment, a moment just before something important was about to be said, and Lila waited expectantly for the words to come rolling out from Halfur's mouth. She also noticed that Halfur's mouth was neither big nor small but constrained in that sort of way like some teachers and certainly her Principal, as nonsense and other forms of unimportant words were just not permitted to get past his teeth or his

ICELAND

lips. So they waited, and just as Halfur was about to let it all out in one big swoosh, Mama said, "Won't you please sit down," and so he did.

He sat in one of the armchairs in the living room. Then Papa sat down and Mama sat down and Lila perched herself next to Mama while Fluffy kept up the nodding and tail wagging and then he did the strangest thing: He winked at Halfur. He then immediately let out a roaring laugh like some storybook elf in one of her fairytale books.

"I have been asked to speak with you," said Halfur. "Not just by the Council of Elders in New York but also at the direction of the Council of Elders in Iceland. Yours was a two Councils kind of problem and we haven't had one of these in years. You see, while we can choose to be invisible or not, we generally do not interact with humans. Fluffy not only caused the interaction but encouraged it, and so we have words not only for the three of you but also for Fluffy." Then he turned to Fluffy and said, "Yes, Fluffy. Don't think that you are going to get off quite so easily here as you caused all of this and you are accountable. The Council wants to know exactly what is on your mind and why this took place."

Fluffy grimaced. Lila had never seen a dog grimace before but she was definitely seeing one do it now. It was the oddest thing to watch. A grimacing dog was something everyone should see once in their life, and here was Lila's moment. Then, Fluffy began to speak but not in English. Lila had heard German before and it wasn't exactly that either but it was some guttural language that was halfway between barking and using the back of your throat to gargle and that was the language he was using to speak to Halfur. Halfur's eyes got big, then even bigger, and Mama and Papa apparently could not understand what Fluffy was saying either because they looked as confused as she was, which was quite confused. Lila was just clueless as Fluffy went on and on and Halfur looked like the kitchen table had just gotten up upon its hind legs and made a speech.

"This changes everything. How were we supposed to know any of this? Why didn't you tell us or at least Ragnar? We have had two Council meetings and a lot of discussion and you never said anything about any of this. And just what is it that you expect us to do now?" asked Halfur. "I had my instructions and I was ready to talk about things with Lila and her parents but now you throw this out and everything has changed. I must go back now and inquire what to do and I really wish you had told us all of this before!"

Halfur then pushed himself up from his chair in the way that bundled people often do in that sort of rolling side to side movement where you push off from the left and then from the right, and he made his way to the door. "I will be back," Halfur said quietly. "I must get new instructions and then we shall see what to do." With that he opened the door, looked first at Fluffy, then at Papa and vanished into the hallway. Literally vanished, but then that is what invisible people do if they like.

Mama had been about to offer Halfur some tea and Papa was waiting expectantly to get to the bottom of the story and Lila was as confused as she had ever been in her young life. Now the three of them sat there, first staring at each other and at Fluffy. Finally, Papa looked quite sternly at Fluffy and said, "Exactly what is going on? I want to know exactly what is going on and I want it in English if you please."

Fluffy looked up at the ceiling and then down at the floor and then anywhere but at Papa and then very softly said, "I am sure you do but I can't tell you quite yet. I apologize but the answer will have to wait."

Lila, who had been standing next to Mama, dropped to the floor. It wasn't exactly a polite dropping or a ladylike dropping but more like a "what do I do now" dropping out of frustration that girls Lila's age do from time to time. They are taught the ladylike stuff, and mostly remember it of course, but there are moments when it just all fades away as emotions overtake good sense. You see, one of the things about being six is that you are just full of emotions that get all tumbled up and then they have no place to go except to be tossed about like you were on a boat in a big sea. When you are older you have stabilizers and larger sails and all manner of things to keep you upright and in control, but at six, well, you just aren't quite there yet. The sails are small, the boat tosses and turns and finally you get up-ended which is why there is such a resemblance to a sack of potatoes dropping to the floor and a six-year-old girl at certain times, and this was one of those times.

"Fluffy, what did you say to Halfur?" Lila said in a very loud voice. A voice so loud that Papa was afraid she would wake their elder neighbor who lived just down the hall. "Fluffy, whatever did you say and why can't you answer Papa's question and why are you being so, so unruly, will you answer that?" The tail stopped wagging and Fluffy hunkered down like Lila was going to flick him on his nose, but she never would of course, and Fluffy looked decidedly unhappy while Lila looked six, not a day over six, and definitely not in control of herself.

"There are things," started Fluffy, "that are not so easy to explain and circumstances not in anyone's control."

This answer caused Lila to get even more annoyed. "Circumstances!" bellowed Lila. "Circumstances are just what...what does that mean and why are you using such big words when you know that I don't understand them? I thought we were friends and I don't know what you are doing at all now." Then Lila started to cry.

Fluffy just hated it when Lila cried, but Mama and Papa even more so, and now everyone was squirming and staring at Lila and no one was happy, not at all. Mama started to bend down to comfort Lila, and Lila edged away and glared at Fluffy amidst the tears, while Papa felt hopelessly out of place and useless. Maybe worse than useless, he wasn't sure, as there were just places men could be of no value and this was one of them.

There are just some secret female places where men are not admitted and this moment contained one of those places, and there was nothing to be done until Lila got ahold of herself and quieted down. So Papa, doing what every man does when confronted by all of this, said nothing and waited. After a time, not as long as some other times in the past, Lila calmed down and scooted herself over towards Mama and waited for Fluffy to say something or another, hopefully in English this time.

"You know the scar on your forearm, Lila? Well, it is not really a scar but a sign, and the sign is the called the sign of the Elven Queen and I know exactly what it is and what it means, and I had to let the invisible people know it was there." The mark, the scar, the sign was clearly on her left forearm, just above her wrist so Lila was not upset with Fluffy, but she didn't like to talk about it much. Maybe people could see it if they looked, she supposed, but it was certainly tucked away at this time of year underneath any outfit that she was wearing. Lila had thought the scar a silly thing all of this time, it had never really concerned her and she had not paid much attention to it. Her mother had seen it of course, but had never mentioned it at all and it was just one of those things that was there but that went unnoticed and unmentioned.

"I'll be back," Lila announced, and off she went to her room. The tears were mostly gone, but off she went in a huff and it was apparent to everyone that she had left to inspect her scar which was something that she had never really given much thought to before now. Lila sat on her bed and now gazed intently at the mark that was just above her wrist. It looked like a scar to her. She had seen other scars on some of the other girls at school when dressing for gym, and she had always just thought it was from some accident of another when they were younger. She had to admit in thinking about it now, that she had always assumed her scar was from some accident when she was much younger and didn't remember it and who cared anyway? She had never cared about it at all except for now. When examining it she wondered just how she had got it. Not to mention, what was all this stuff about some Elven Queen?

She knew what a queen was, the ladies that got to wear tiaras and crowns and fancy party dresses all day. She also knew that they were the mothers of the princesses that she often dreamed about, but what an Elven Queen was befuddled her. Then she rushed back into the living room and asked, "Mama, what is an Elven Queen, when did I get this scar, and do you really think it is some strange mark on my arm?"

Mama explained, quietly, softly, that Lila had been born with the mark on her forearm, that she had always had it and that it was called a birthmark by people. Mama also said that she knew no more than Lila about Elven Queens and that while they had both read about them in some of Lila's books, that she didn't know much more than that. Lila then turned to Papa and started to ask the same questions. Papa gained some control back and said that he had no information about Elven Queens either, but that he could attest to the fact that she had been born with this birthmark which was all that he knew.

Then they all turned and looked at Fluffy, who said, "It is the mark of the Elven Queen, of that there is no doubt, I can see it and it has not been on a person in more than two thousand years, but only on the invisible people." That was why he had first taken Lila to see Ragnar. Not that Ragnar could have seen it of course, he didn't have the spectacles, but you can generally sense these things when they are there and Fluffy had hoped that Ragnar would pick up the scent, which was doggish for "pick up on it." This had not happened, now Fluffy knew, but perhaps because it was so unsuspected to be found on a human girl. When this mark appears on a girl, any sort of girl, it causes all kinds of commotion and all kinds of consequences and all sorts of jumble for the invisible people. "This is a very serious thing," Fluffy explained, "and there are generations where one is not found or seen by anyone, and to find one on Lila was, well, something so startling and unexpected that something had to be done. There was just no other choice!"

CHAPTER 13
WHAT COMES AFTER NEXT

Papa had gone to work. It wasn't that far away, Lila knew, but it was far enough that he wasn't there. Halfur had just showed up yesterday and tossed Lila and her parents into a great whirlwind of looking up things on the Internet, checking out every Elven Queen they could find and eventually concluding that while the Internet might be good for some things, that this was not one of them. The information was sketchy or a bunch of "gobbly gook," said Mama, whatever that was or meant, but in any event, not much that was useful was found. It was a lot of stuff said by someone, told to them by someone else, and rumors tossed about by people no one had ever heard of, so most

of what they had found was dismissed. It was easy to find "birthmark" and Lila now thought she knew what they were, but what some birthmark indicated or meant was not to be found on any of those doctor's sites that they had looked up.

Lila was glad that she was born with it and that it wasn't some scar from some accident, but that was about her only feeling on the subject. She had now examined it three times and she had even allowed Mama to look closely at it but neither of them could make anything out of it at all. The birthmark was red and yellow with something bluish on top of it with some jagged squiggles, but that was all that could be seen. Lila had thought, at first, that it was bad and then not so bad, and finally that she had it so she might as well get used to the fact that it was there.

Mama and Lila were sitting at the computer and just about to try a different site that they had found to get information, when there came another ringing of the doorbell without an announcement of anyone coming. Lila jumped, Mama jumped higher, and the doorbell rang again. Mama went to the door and politely said, "Who is it?"

The answer was a very sweet, feminine, faint and

calm, "Hildur."

Now this being New York City and life being what it is, Mama peeked through the little hole in the door to get a glimpse of their visitor. First there was nothing to be seen, but then *poof,* there was woman standing there. If the going from nothing to something wasn't startling enough, then the woman that Mama was staring at was not what one sees every day. She was wearing a long blue puffy dress that looked like it was made from satin or maybe silk, a fluffy blond head of hair with two twinkling blue eyes set right below them, a smile that lit up the hallway and a wand that twinkled and beamed as if it had a life of its own. This was hardly what one sees wandering the streets of New York in the wintertime, and Mama looked at it all and opened the door and said, "Hildur, please come in."

Hildur had gotten a step, just one step into the doorway, when Lila came charging out from the living room and started spewing words like they would never stop, which is sometimes the way of it with a six-year-old girl. "Oh my gosh, oh my gosh! Are you a queen? You must be a queen, Oh, I just love your dress and oh my gosh! Is that a crown on your head?

You are so tall, how did you get to be so tall?" Then, before Hildur could get one word out edgewise into all of Lila's words, Lila began again, "Oh my gosh, you must be in the movies or you are a famous model. And what is on your head? Is that a crown and is that a wand? Is it really a wand and does it work like do magic or something?" Lila then grabbed Hildur's hand and pulled her and tugged her into the living room and asked her to sit down before Mama had a chance to do anything or say anything, because Lila had taken up all of the space that was available for inviting someone into your house properly.

Then Mama looked at Hildur and Hildur looked at Mama and they both started to laugh. They had both been six-year-old girls once and the memory must have floated back into their heads just then because they both just sat there and laughed like the best joke ever had just been told, a polite one of course, and neither one could stop laughing. Lila looked at Mama and then looked at Hildur in such a manner that she had no idea why they were laughing so hard, because while the two women had once been six, poor Lila and never been any older than six and could not imagine what was going on between the two older females.

"I am so sorry," said Mama. "Lila gets a little excited from time to time and I apologize for her whisking you into the living room in that fashion."

"You need not worry about a thing," said Hildur. "Your daughter was quite polite and yes, she is a bundle of energy, but what a delightful child and I couldn't be more pleased to be here. It was quite a decision for me to be here, you know," she said, knowing that she didn't know of course, but she felt like she should say something about this. "And I wasn't sure for a moment if you were going to let me in. Yet here we are and this is a big day and I am sure you have lots of questions, because I have a lot of them to ask you too."

Lila then bounded over to Hildur, bounded would be the only good word for it, and grabbed her hand and asked her once again if she was a queen. Then before Hildur could answer, Lila said, "You know what I mean, one of those good queens in my storybooks, not one of the bad ones like the one with the mirror or something, because you are just so beautiful that I am sure you are not one of those old and ugly queens."

The room then noticeably brightened from the sparkle in Hildur's eyes, and she answered that there was a queen, who was her mother, and that she was just a princess and not nearly old enough to be queen in any event. "Oh my gosh! A princess, a real princess, and you are in our apartment and sitting with me and Mama! Oh my gosh! This must be the best day ever because Mama and I have never met a princess before, or at least I haven't and I don't think Mama has either. Have you, Mama?"

Mama just shook her head and then thought of what she must do now. So she asked Hildur if she would like some tea and Hildur said, "That would be fine." So off Mama went to the kitchen.

Lila was about to speak and say something of great importance, she was sure, when Hildur put her finger to her lips, her very bright red lips, and said, "Let's just wait for your mother to come back and then we can discuss whatever you like." So Lila sat there and waited, and presently Mama arrived with the tea in their very best little blue and white teacups, and they all took a sip and Lila thought of her own tea parties with her dolls but this was so much better, oh so much better, having tea with a real princess.

"I hope that Ragnar and Halfur were quite polite with both of you," started Hildur. "The invisible men

can be quite abrupt sometimes, whether in Iceland or New York, and, well, you know how men can be after all. It is not their fault, of course, as they are just men but I do hope they were at least polite."

"Oh everyone was just delightful, nothing to apologize for, nothing at all," said Mama. "I am sure they didn't know quite what to make of us, and I must admit that we didn't know quite what to make of them but the circumstances were just a little odd as you might imagine. It is not often that Lila and Papa and I meet invisible people, and I suppose that your friends don't socialize much with us either so it was just a tad bit awkward and nothing more. It seems that Fluffy had all of this planned out long before, but then he told us nothing about any of this, and so we just kind of went along with what it seemed he wanted to do. But then I am sure that he had his own good reasons. Fluffy is very kind, without question, and I have no doubt that he has Lila's best interests at heart."

"Ah yes, Fluffy," said the Princess. "Yes, he is quite kind and quite well known and he is a good-hearted dog and something even more than that, which we can discuss when the time is right. So first things being first, and one of the reasons that I am here and not someone else, I would like to see Lila's birthmark, if that is possible. We would not send a man to do this of course, that just wouldn't do, and then given the very special nature of Lila's birthmark it was decided by the Council that I should be the one to come here and verify its existence. If that is alright with you, of course," said Hildur looking at Mama.

Lila then leapt up and plopped herself right onto the lap of the Princess and thrust out her left arm and showed the birthmark above her wrist to Hildur. The Princess looked at it, examined it you might say, and then opened her purse. It was just kind of a purse really. It looked more like a dark blue velvet bag tied together at the top with a silk rope. Then she took out some spectacles. They were nothing like Mama had ever seen. They had large gold rims with what appeared to be very soft blue sapphire lenses and they had sparkly things which seemed to float in the crystal. The Princess slipped them on, well kind of, as they were perching right in the middle of her nose as she examined the birthmark. Then she then looked at Mama and said quite simply, "Yes, that is it. I can make it out quite distinctly. It shows the mountains of Iceland on a bright sunny day, with the Elven Crown glistening, and the mountains are inside the crown and set against a crystal clear sky," said Princess Hildur. "It is quite unbelievable really

and it hasn't been seen on a human girl in thousands of years, but most assuredly, that is it. It is now what to do about it that remains the question, and that is a really big question for my people, as no one alive has been confronted with such a question before.

"You see, my mother and her mother before that and going oh so far back are the descendants of the last human that had the sign of the Elven Queen. Our family has ruled the kingdom for these many centuries all because of her. So you see it is not just our people, but my own mother and I that have to figure out not only what this means but what to do about it. Quite frankly, none of us are quite sure what to do about this at all. It is a startling event that must also have startled the people thousands of years ago, but then here we are now and we have scholars consulting our history to try to make sense of all of this. The first answer is easy, the birthmark is there and real, but the other questions that it raises are oh so many and oh so complicated that great thought must be put into answering them correctly."

Mama shook her head in that knowing kind of way that only mothers can understand. Lila looked befuddled, Hildur shook her head along with Mama's,

and a great quiet descended upon the room. Fluffy poked his head from around the couch, looked at them both and smiled. Now normally, when a dog bears his teeth it is an aggressive sort of thing, but this was not one of those looks, it was a smile and of that Lila was certain. The Princess looked at Fluffy and sighed and sighed some more, and said, "Now Fluffy, what have you gotten us into this time?" But Fluffy said nothing and seemed quite content with himself that he had opened the door, even if he was not the one to do the deciding. "You see," Hildur said, looking directly at Mama, "Fluffy is quite old, older than anyone as far as I know, and it was Fluffy that also found my great, great, I don't know how many greats really, grandmother, who was the first queen of my family's reign. And here we are again and it is so very confusing."

"Family can be confusing," said Mama, "very confusing." Now here was a situation that she had never encountered before, and then she thought of Lila and laughed, and she said to the Princess, "Lila would call this a number over sixty kind of problem," and they both laughed together even though their heads both hurt from thinking about it.

Chapter 14
Old Dogs and New Tricks

Princess Hildur had left her wand, well it looked like a wand to Lila, on the table next to her chair. Just as everyone was thinking about family and the difficulties that sometimes came with them, the wand began to glow a bright blue. Mama looked at Hildur and pointed at it, and the Princess put her hand to her mouth and said, "Oh my. I must be going, I am so sorry as I intended to stay longer, but I have to go now. There is nothing else I can do."

Lila was sad to see the Princess leave so soon but knew there must be some good reason for it, so she jumped up and said, "So nice to have met you." Then she remembered something from one of her books and said, "Am I supposed to curtsy or something? I have seen the pictures but I am not exactly sure how it is done."

Every smile that had ever been smiled in the living room could not match the smile upon the face of the Princess. "Yes, Lila, I suppose you are," she said. "But then I am not sure as one princess does not need to curtsy to another princess, and we are not yet quite sure exactly who you are or how you fit in to everything. I will be back," she promised, "and then we all may know more." With that, the door opened, Hildur vanished, and Mama sat down to wonder about what would happen to Lila and to their family. It had been a big day and Papa wasn't even home yet, and what would he say?

Lila was also thinking but she was looking at Fluffy and he had that very distinct, "I know but I am not going to tell you yet" look that people get sometimes, dogs almost never, but here they were.

The rest of the afternoon was pleasant enough. No more surprises. No more guessing games, and then Papa was home from work.

"Papa, oh Papa, guess who visited us today. A princess, a real princess," gushed Lila.

"What, what do you mean, what princess? Where is your mother and what are you talking about?" Papa asked.

"Well, she had on this sequined blue dress, or maybe they were diamonds since she was a princess, and she had a wand and she looked at my birthmark and said it was real and she had tea with Mama and I and, oh my gosh, Papa, I have never met a real princess before have you?" Papa shook his head, he did that sometimes as if clearing out cobwebs or odd thoughts that tend to come into one's mind sometimes, and he looked somewhat confused as he looked for Mama so she could clear all of this up.

"So where is your mother?" Papa asked Lila, and she pointed at the kitchen which is a place mothers sometime go to sort things out. Lila had learned at four, or maybe it was five, that mothers sometimes putter or clean up rooms or houses when things were somewhat uncertain. Mothers just tend to retreat to these occupations as a matter of course, and then when asked about something they can say, "Don't you see I am cleaning?" so they do not have to get involved with things which they have no wish to be involved with, which was the case at the moment

for Mama.

Papa made directly for the kitchen to inquire about what had gone on today, and was met with exactly what Lila guessed, "Can't you see I am cleaning? I will be done shortly and I will tell you all about today, but now I am cleaning so you must just wait." Now Papa was not dumb—no one had ever accused him of being dumb and he was also a good father and a good husband, and so he had learned long ago when to retreat, which is exactly what he did. In the living room there was a chair, not unlike a given chair in most houses, that belonged to Papa, and that is what he made for and upon arriving, he plopped down.

Lila, of course, watched the whole thing, and plopped was exactly the right word for it. Lila had been taught to be graceful, to be ladylike always, but men, well, they were allowed to plop and no one gave it a second thought. Lila only considered it for a few moments and then she thought of the boys in school who were her own age, and she decided that Papa's plop was so much nicer that theirs when they sat down which was really more like a thud, and so she gave Papa the credit he deserved. Not that it really mattered; Papa was Papa after all, but it

was nice to know that he did better than those very aggravating monkeys at school who were just awful. She wondered why no one had ever taught them to be civilized. Papa smiled at Lila and Lila smiled back, and they both waited for Mama to appear.

Papa sat there and thought how peaceful life had been before they went out on their quest to knock on cornerstones in downtown New York. There had been no invisible people, Fluffy had been around but in a not quite real or believable sort of way and the normal problems of everyday life were all that concerned him. Papa thought it was amazing how pleasant and simple those small problems were, and he wondered about the problems he may now have to face and what size they might be. He could not imagine yet, as Mama had not informed him, but he would face whatever was necessary because what else was there to do?

Mama finally emerged from the kitchen. She had that "I have done what is needed to be done" look on her face as she sat down and turned to Papa. "Well, dear. How was your day?" she said, as if that was really all there was to say and today had been just like any other day.

143

Papa would have none of it, though. "Oh no you don't. My day was just fine but your day was off the charts I hear, and let's hear about that first."

Mama smiled and said, "Yes, dear, whatever you like," which was always the safest choice in moments like this, and Mama had undergone enough excitement for one day, thank you.

"You see," said Mama, "there was a knock at the door and a princess arrived. She even looked like a princess out of one of Lila's story books and when I went to the door, there was no one there, and then there was someone there and it was a princess named Hildur. I don't know about you, perhaps before you married me you met a princess, but I had never met one before and it was difficult to know quite what to do or how to behave, but I did my best. We had tea and she examined Lila's birthmark, and she told the most amazing story about how the birthmark was real, that it had not been seen on a human for several thousand years when it had first appeared in her family, and that Fluffy was the one that found them both."

Papa asked, "What, what, what do you mean that Fluffy found them both if the first one was several

thousand years ago?"

Mama looked down then up and said, "Yes, there is that, and it is so confusing just like it has been every day since we first met the invisible people. We were going to talk about it and then her wand, or scepter, or whatever it is that queens and princesses wave about, turned blue and glowed like some diamond when the light shines through it, and then she had to go and so we never made it to that part of the discussion."

Papa just sat there. He had no idea what you were supposed to do when some storybook came alive, and he had not even read this one. Perhaps there was a script here, but he assuredly didn't know it nor did he quite know what to do about it. "Where is Fluffy?" Papa asked. Two bright blue eyes peeked out from around the chair and a whole mane of black and white fur could be seen on a head and a neck that popped out. "How is this possible?" asked Papa. "And just what are you doing? Please tell me."

One blue eye closed and then the other closed and there was a look of some concentration on Fluffy's face. "I wasn't always a dog you see, or perhaps you don't, but it is quite convenient to retain this form as it solves ever so many problems."

That is what Fluffy said, or perhaps announced would be more accurate. "So are you going to tell us what you are or were?" asked Papa. "And explain how you have lived so long and just how old are you anyway?"

There was more eye closing and opening, and then Fluffy stared out into the distance and said, "No, I don't think I will. This is not the right time for it nor the right place for it, and the answer would set all kinds of things in motion for which I am not ready. So I am afraid that the answer is going to have to be 'no' for the present."

Papa shuffled about in his chair and then said, "I see," when he didn't at all, but then he didn't know quite what else to say so he said that and left it there.

Night had fallen or maybe dropped in because neither Papa or Mama had noticed it when it came. Lila had gone to bed, Fluffy was in Lila's room, and a stillness had entered the house. It is a funny thing about having a six-year-old—there was rarely any stillness to be found, and when it was, it was after Lila had gone to bed. So Mama and Papa sat there quietly when Mama asked, "What do you make of all of this?" and Papa just looked at her.

"I have no idea how we got here, where this is going, or how it will end—if there is an ending to be had. I remember Alice and how she fell down a rabbit hole and I would be quite happy if our story was as simple as that, but somehow, and perhaps because I am part of it, I am not sure just what is coming next. I never thought I would be a character in a storybook and was not prepared to be one. Yet here I am, and here you are, and we have Lila, an ancient dog, or something or someone of unknown origin, a princess slipping about, invisible people living in cornerstones of buildings and all manners of things which I was not trained for or had even thought about and yet here we are," Papa said and sighed. "On that note I am awfully tired and I am going to bed in the hope that when I wake up the world will make sense once again," and then Papa padded off to bed.

CHAPTER 15
THE MORNING CHANGED NOTHING

Papa woke up. He was in his pajamas in his own room, in their apartment in New York City, and he looked around like something might have changed during the night, but it had not. He hadn't expected it to really, and while he might have wished for a return to the times before Fluffy and the invisible people that surrounded him, he was not hopeful. Work had been important once but now it hardly mattered, and while someone might know what was in store for him and his family, he did not know them, and did not expect any immediate answer. So he got up and stretched and went to brush his teeth because that is what papas do the first thing in the morning, at least this papa.

Lila had been bundled off to school and Papa had left for work and Mama was doing her general puttering, and she wondered aloud who might show up today. "A king, an emperor, a sea sprite, it could be almost anything or anyone," said Mama to no one, and yet she was happy, she supposed, that whoever had come had knocked at the front door and not just popped into the living room unannounced. Invisible people or animals could do that she guessed, and at least the people that she had met had all been quite polite.

"We should talk," said Fluffy.

Mama looked at Fluffy, who had not spoken much recently and had denied Papa's request for more information, and just said, "Okay." She wandered into the living room, sat down, looked at Fluffy who had also planted himself on the rug there and said, "Okay, Fluffy. What is on your mind?"

"Well, you know the birthmark that is on Lila's forearm. It is not just some trivial thing and I thought you should know that. The Princess explained part of it to you, but you see, it changes everything and not only for Lila, but for all of the invisible people

in all of the kingdom. This is why the problem is so vexing. They have a queen, who is liked well enough, the king died quite some time ago, and they have a princess who is very well thought of and who will inherit the crown one day. Then all of a sudden, Lila shows up with her birthmark and the invisible people don't know what to make of it. Whether you know it or not, the entire kingdom is in turmoil because of it. Whether it is in the cornerstones of the downtown buildings or in the boulders in Central Park, or the whole of Iceland where they come from, no one is talking about anything other than Lila and her birthmark and what should be done. The world, for the invisible people, has gone topsy-turvy, and so I thought you should know this," said Fluffy.

Mama looked at Fluffy. She said, "What about our world? Don't you think it is has gone topsy-turvy for us too? Don't you think that meeting invisible dogs, people, and having all of this shoved in our lap has changed our lives? We were all quite normal before, all settled in a pleasant life and then, poof, the world changed. And what are we supposed to do about it?" Mama asked.

"Yes, there is that," Fluffy mumbled. "Yes, there

is that."

Just then, as Mama was about to go on, there was a knock at the front door. Well, almost a knock, it was more like a tap, and a not very energetic one at that. Mama went to the front door, peeked through the little hole and, seeing Heidi, opened it of course. Heidi, Ragnar's daughter, stood with her blond hair swirling everywhere, looking sheepish and not really comfortable being there or being seen. Then Heidi curtsied, well kind of curtsied, more like a half bow as she was trying to be polite, but apparently had not been taught this maneuver too well.

Heidi said, "Well, er um, ah…I have brought something for you all and Lila." She was holding a silver platter, a small round one that looked like a family heirloom as it had scrolls and whirls and all kinds of fancy etchings. On it was a note. "Is Lila here?" asked Heidi.

"No, she is at school," Mama told her.

"Oh yes, of course. What was I thinking?" responded Heidi. "Well, this is for you and Lila's father and Lila too, of course," she said as she pushed the platter out towards Mama. "We would all be pleased if you could attend. Actually it is very important that

you attend and we will be looking forward to seeing you soon. I have been instructed to give this to you by my father and others, and I am to wait for an answer."

Mama, always thinking of Heidi as being quite nice, invited her in. They sat down and then Mama looked at the note. The envelope was in that cream color that one sees in stationary stores that are used for important occasions. The lettering was some kind of script that could only be drawn by someone very artistic or by someone schooled in writing these kinds of notes. The envelope was addressed to "Lila and her Parents," but it was so scrolled and flowery that it was somewhat difficult to read. Then Mama turned the note over and there was a red wax seal with a crown etched over a boulder, which Mama thought must be something of great importance, though she just wasn't sure what exactly.

Mama smiled and opened the note only to discover that it was an invitation and for this Saturday. They were all invited to "Boulder I, Parliament House" for lunch by the Most High Council of Elders to dine with the Queen and the Princess and the Royal Court. Mama's eyes widened, *What should I wear?* was the first thing that came into her mind, because while she was a Mama, she was also a female, and this is what females think first when these sorts of things happen. Mama had traveled some with Papa and had been to many nice restaurants and so forth, but she had never been invited to a royal lunch. A quick assessment of her closet yielded nothing at all suitable, and then she turned to Heidi and said, "What does one wear to this sort of thing?"

"Just any old thing will be fine I am sure," said Heidi, but Mama knew differently. Just any old thing would not do at all, and this would entail a trip to a high class store. No, several stores, where just the right outfit must be chosen. While Papa would not be happy with the cost, he would just have to get over it, and that is exactly what Mama told herself. Then she would also have to get a new dress for Lila, something elegant, something charming. What did young girls wear to these sorts of things? Mama knew that Heidi was not going to be of much help. Then she thought of Papa's suits, he owned a number of them but nothing for an occasion like this, and she would have to march him off to a suitable suit maker and supervise the choice of a new suit which is exactly what mamas do when the event is important.

"I certainly will not leave it to him," Mama said, as he could end up in some mixture of plaid and stripes. He could embarrass himself all that he liked at work, but when she was present, well, that was a very different story, as he would find out. Now all of this took place in a few brief moments because it had to be hashed out in Mama's mind before she could respond to Heidi. Once she had set the stage however, she was ready to give an answer.

"Yes, of course we shall all be there," she told Heidi. She had no idea what Papa might have had planned for lunch on Saturday, but Mama was not, was absolutely not, going to miss lunch with a Council of Elders and a queen and a princess under any circumstances. She had dreamed of dining with these sorts of people since she was a little girl, and she was not going to let the opportunity pass her by. Now to be honest, she had never thought that the opportunity would ever come to pass, but now that it was here she was going to take it!

Heidi looked pleased and she blinked in and out of existence several times and then said, "I shall tell them then that you will be attending."

"Now, Heidi," said Mama, "you must tell me, what

do people wear to these sorts of lunches?"

Heidi flicked her head this way and that, the mane of long her blond hair that somewhat resembled a lion's in both fuzziness and furriness, was whisked about. She pondered the question in the way that many young girls do when they aren't sure of the answer. "I honestly don't know," she said. "I have never been to one of these luncheons and I was not invited to this one, but I will try to find out for you and let you know."

Mama nodded and said, "Well, you can just call me on the phone when you have an answer. No need to waste time and money for you to come uptown yourself." Heidi looked at Mama and laughed and laughed until you might have thought that something would get broken in the room.

"We don't have phones, you know, and we don't have money either," Heidi said. "But I will get an answer to you one way or another."

Mama looked at Heidi in a very perplexed way. "What do you mean you don't have money?" asked Mama. "How do you pay for things?"

Heidi grinned and said, "Oh, we just sign for things and then we settle up once a year on New Year's

Day in gemstones. You know, diamonds and rubies and emeralds and things like that, and we balance the accounts."

Mama stared at Heidi, "What do you do if you don't have enough of those things to pay the bills?"

Heidi smiled and said, "Oh that is easy. We keep records and then go mining in December to get ready for Settling Day and so it all gets taken care of in a very pleasant fashion, which seems so much easier than the way you do things. Well, I must go home now. I have schoolwork to do and I have to clean my room my mother said, so I must go home." With that Heidi winked out of existence and was gone as Mama reflected upon the usefulness of doors and decided that they were not so useful after all.

CHAPTER 16

AN ANSWER

It was just about three hours later when Mama got her answer. She had gone into the kitchen to make some tea when she saw a piece of paper lying next to the toaster. It was marked, "Miss Lila's Mother," so she knew it was for her. How it got there or when it came was a total mystery, but what else was new? So Mama took her tea and sat down at the kitchen table and read the note.

It said, "Velvet, I asked my mother and that is all she said and that is all I know." The note was signed "Heidi." Mama pondered this. She thought and thought about it and finally concluded that her dress and Lila's dress would be made of velvet, and Papa could wear one of those tuxedo jackets that were made of velvet, and that this would get them through the luncheon without embarrassment. At least Heidi's answer was something; not what she had hoped for and a little more description would have been useful, but it was helpful nonetheless.

It was later that day, after Lila had returned from school and Papa had gotten home from work, that she told them both the exciting news. She told them about Heidi and about their upcoming lunch and that velvet was the attire. Lila was quite delighted with this as dressing up was always fun. Usually though, she dressed up to play pretend, but now she got to dress up for real and there was something quite exciting about that. Papa, however, was not so sure, and while he owned a tuxedo it was not a velvet one, but he assured Mama that what he had would just be fine.

Mama shook her head and said, "Absolutely not," in the way that only a mother or a wife can say it. Then, when Papa started to say something else, he got that withering look that could take the petals off of a rose, and so he decided against saying anything more. He hunkered down to the reality that he would

have to do as told and so that was just that. Much easier to go along, he decided, much easier.

Papa wanted to look at the note, and so Mama handed the envelope to him. "There is only one problem," he announced. "We have been invited to 'Boulder I, Parliament House,' and where the heck is that?" Then something struck him and he said, "What if this is some rock in Iceland? How would we get there?" He fervently hoped that this was not the case because while it was cold in New York it must be colder in Iceland, and he really didn't want to dine in some boulder in Iceland during the dead of winter.

Mama said, "Oh, I am sure not. It must be somewhere in Central Park where the rest of the invisible people live." She hoped she was right. Just then, in the nick of time, as if it had all been planned somehow, another piece of paper fell from the envelope. It was a drawing of Central Park with some roads and streams and lakes and large rocks and a big X marked upon a particularly big boulder. Underneath it there was some writing that said "Boulder I" so the problem was solved before it had hardly begun.

Relief, thought Papa. *What a relief!*

The rest of the week went quietly enough. No big problems, no other visits, and the shopping had not been all that painful. Mama and Lila had gone to this store and that store and tried on all kinds of velvet dresses and gowns in all kinds of colors. They had finally settled on a dark brown dress for Lila with puffy sleeves that settled in at about the knees. Mama had chosen a red velvet dress that was mid-calf and quite conservative in its make-up. There would be nothing sexy for this occasion, matters of State and all, and she wanted to give a good impression from the beginning of a mother that took good care of her child and her husband. That was the look that she tried to emulate in her dress.

Papa had somewhat more difficulty, but nothing that could not be handled. He had gone to several tuxedo stores and one department store that carried tuxedos, but to no avail. He felt that he looked like a puff ball or some kind of French pastry in what he had tried on, and that would never do at all. He had never attempted to wear velvet before and while the fabric was quite good for the female gender, he was most assuredly not of that gender and had no experience with wearing velvet as part of any of his attire. He came home and made a brief stab at convincing

Mama that the tuxedo that he owned was just fine. Upon receiving a second withering stare, out he went again into the cold and snow and tried another store. He had found one online that promised to "Suit for Royalty," and while he had never heard of the place before, off he went.

Upon arrival at this place, which smelled somewhat like a gentleman's club in London that reeked faintly of expensive cigar smoke, he felt more at home. Mr. Boonlsby was the proprietor and he rushed over to Papa as he edged out some salesman that was heading Papa's way. "May I help you, sir? There must be an important occasion no doubt if you are coming into my establishment."

Papa said, "Yes, an affair of State in Central Park, for which I must be properly attired and I was thinking of a velvet tuxedo coat or velvet smoking jacket or something of the sort."

Mr. Boonisby stopped and looked at Papa very hard. "It wouldn't be a luncheon this Saturday would it? It couldn't be that could it, sir?" said Mr. Boonisby quite directly.

Papa, who had been looking at the various racks of suits and so forth, turned on his heel quick as a

dormouse and said, "Yes, that is exactly what it could be. And how do you know anything about that?"

Mr. Boonisby grinned faintly as someone who knows a thing or two is apt to do, and said, "Yes, sir. I do know a thing or two about it, and we have had many refined gentlemen in and out the past two days also looking for the appropriate clothes for this event. We have a number of signatures for Settlement Day, but I am sure you would know nothing about that. Or would you?"

Papa, who now held the "I know a thing or two" card, grinned back faintly and said, "That I might, that I just might." This was a dance that men do sometimes. How much do you know and how much should I tell you that I know? What came next was quite appropriate for a men's high-end suit shop. It was called the sizing up.

So Mr. Boonisby regarded Papa, and Papa looked the proprietor up and down, and finally Mr. Boonisby said to Papa, "Why don't you come this way and sit down? The store is somewhat more crowded than you might be accustomed to, even though it doesn't seem that way."

There was not a wink, not exactly a wink, that

164

accompanied this statement, but it was awfully close
to one. Papa followed Mr. Boonisby to a room just off
the main suiting room and the two of them sat down.
The chairs were green leather and quite comfortable
and looked like they had been there for uncountable
years just welcoming the posteriors of gentlemen
looking for a particular something. "You came in by
the front door, you may have noticed," Mr. Boonisby
said. "About a third of our customers come in by that
door," he said. Then he pointed to another door at

the back of the room and said to Papa, "The rest of our customers come in by this door. It has not been opened in decades and we keep it locked, but they come in that way nonetheless. While no doorbell is rung or knock heard, still they come in looking for that something special." Then Mr. Boonisby placed his hands together, laced his fingers, put them on his rather rotund stomach and said, "You are not the father of Lila by any chance, are you?"

Papa's eyes got as round as snowballs, maybe rounder. Papa then blinked and nodded and was not sure at all what to say next, when Mr. Boonisby interceded and said, "It is fine, all fine. Just a matter of getting used to it and then knowing what to do about it. You have stumbled into the right establishment, which is fortunate for you. You are the talk of this particular group of people, you know. All the rage, and they have been speaking of nothing else for weeks since you first met Ragnar."

It had never occurred to Papa that other individuals had met these people. It had never entered his mind at all. "But why not?" he asked himself. "Why would his family be the only ones that had met the invisible people? They did need clothes to wear, he supposed,

when they could be seen or when their friends looked at them so it made sense, quite good sense if you thought about it."

"Now, I cannot say too much," said Mr. Boonisby. "A matter of propriety and all, and I am sure you understand that there are matters, certain delicate matters, that should avoid discussion."

Papa nodded, being somewhat a man of the world, well at least a man of New York, and said, "Of course." Mr. Boonisby also nodded, and an agreement had been reached.

Then the proprietor said, "The good news is that I can outfit you properly for your important event, though you may find the style somewhat, well, Renaissance might be the word, but then these people are from Iceland originally, you know, and so certain allowances must be made."

A knowing smile lit up both faces as sometimes happens when a secret is shared, and Papa said, "I shall leave it to you then and trust your judgment as this luncheon is quite important to my wife and daughter, and I don't wish to disappoint either of them."

Several hours later, after multiple pinnings and

fittings and more harrumph and trouble than had ever appended a suit bought by Papa, the outfit was cut and agreed upon. The jacket was made of red velvet with rather wide lapels, and the pants were of black velvet without cuffs and the shirt was somewhat more starchy than Papa's taste with a collar that no one had worn in this century. This was the fashion, he was told, and so he went along with the plan. Papa was then assured that his clothes would be delivered Thursday afternoon or Friday morning, and then Mr. Boonisby inquired as to what Mama and Lila would be wearing. Papa told him and then the proprietor blanched and said, "That will never do, never do at all."

He went on, "My wife owns an establishment for women and she is also acquainted with our mutual friends, and perhaps you may wish to direct them there. Just a thought, you know, just a suggestion. But then if your wife and daughter wish to be properly attired, it is one that you might mention to them. What you have described just will not do and your wife will be quite unhappy if she intends to make the proper impression, which women always do as you may have noticed." There were more knowing nods and that quiet agreement that traverses from one

man of the world to the next. They shook hands and Papa left the store to head back uptown.

It was early afternoon and Mama and Lila were at home when Papa entered. They were engaged in some sort of lively discussion between themselves and with Lila's dolls. Something not infrequent, Papa had observed, and then he sat down and told Mama about his experience. Well you could not believe the fluttering that took place.

"Lila, you must change and we must leave immediately and we have to return our dresses and then go downtown and we must leave now, immediately, and do not waste one second." Lila began to say something and then she noticed that look of determination in Mama's eyes, and off she flew to her bedroom.

She appeared some minutes later as Mama stood there tapping her foot, and Mama took one look at her and said, "Oh, Lila. What are you doing in your blue jeans? That will never do. Never, never, never."

Lila, looking somewhat bewildered, looked at Mama and said, "But Mama, Papa was in his blue jeans when he went to the clothing store and what is wrong with what I am wearing?"

Mama looked aghast. "Haven't I taught you any better than this? Papa is well, you know, a man," and she may have well said something more than that to her daughter had they been alone, but that was enough to say now as she smiled politely at Papa, so off Lila went back to her bedroom. More minutes passed, more time flew and then Lila appeared again in a suitable dress. At least she hoped it was a suitable dress, and it seemed to be because Mama grabbed her hand and, after bundling up with their velvet dresses in hand to be returned, out the door they went. Luckily, it was just a subway ride downtown to the shop of Mrs. Boonisby.

Upon arriving at the shop, Mama politely asked for Mrs. Boonisby. A somewhat round but very jovial woman came out of the backroom and said, "One moment please, I am fitting someone. Please sit down and make yourself comfortable." Mama looked about and she didn't see other clients in the dress shop nor did she hear any conversation, until she heard one of the salesladies say something. But there was no reply, and then Mama realized the reason for the rather lopsided conversation and knew she was at the right place.

Mama and Lila sat down. They were perched in nice flowery chairs that looked as if they had belonged to Queen Victoria and probably had or should have. Mama thought they were just perfect for the shop. As Mama looked about, she noticed that the all clothing was different from anything she had seen recently in the magazines that came in the mail. The dresses on the racks were not being shown in any of them. Mama prided herself on keeping up with the latest fashions, but here were dresses that matched the chairs, something from the era of Queen Victoria or maybe even before that, she just wasn't sure. "Odd, quite odd," Mama said to herself. They looked more like the dresses that Lila used for pretend dinners with princesses, but then it dawned on Mama that they were going to have lunch with a real princess and not a pretend one either, even if so few people knew about her.

"One moment, one moment, be right there," called Mrs. Boonisby from the other room. "I am just finishing up and it is so difficult with these people as they wink in and then they wink out and you don't want to stick them and it is ever so much more work." Mama and Lila politely waited, fidgeting around some, but perched like ladies on their chairs like they were supposed to. Finally, Mrs. Boonisby made her appearance.

"The clothes you have here," said Mama. "They look like something from another century. You must own a vintage store I suppose."

Mrs. Boonisby smiled and then finally giggled as she seemed to be searching for the right response and then said, "Oh no, it is just that our special clients like to dress in a certain way in keeping with their traditions, and so we try to comply with their wishes. It is a matter of respect, you know, and well, frankly, it is good business." Mama smiled. She got that, and she explained, "Yes, that is why we are here. We understand that you deal in these sorts of things, and neither Lila nor I want to be out of place at this lunch that we have been invited to on Saturday. That would never do, not at all."

That Mrs. Boonisby understood perfectly, she assured Mama. "One needs to be attired in the correct clothes for this kind of occasion," said Mrs. Boonisby. "While you may not know it, given your position, all eyes will certainly be on you and Lila as no one has seen a young lady marked with the sign of the Elven Queen in such a very long time. You may claim it is a

birthmark and they will all smile at you quite politely, but they will not believe it. To them it is something much more than that. Then, there is the matter of who will be in attendance. The Council of Elders does not meet often. They only gather for significant affairs of State or some disaster or when the Queen or Princess requests it. It is not often that they hold a formal lunch, and it is considered a Crown Affair and a very important occurrence. Without question, this is the right store for you and at the right moment. I am ever so glad that you are here."

"Well, we shall trust in your judgment," said Mama. "Usually I have a sense for this sort of thing, but I have no sense about this at all and so we shall follow your advice."

Mrs. Boonisby nodded and said, "I was thinking about something in burgundy for Lila, velvet of course, and with a black off-set in silk going around the hem, and then some black embroidery around the collar as the perfect dress for your lunch. Something demure in fashion but not too showy is just the right dress for the occasion. Our friends will probably inspect her up and down and I think this is entirely fitting for any such inspections."

Mama, looking none too sure, nodded and said, "But can you have this all done by Thursday or Friday at the latest? Lunch is this Saturday, you know."

Now Mrs. Boonisby, quite used to this sort of thing in her profession, said, "Oh yes, no trouble at all, and I will have it delivered to your apartment." Measurements were then taken and pins were used in large quantities on the burgundy dress in stock.

So at least that much is settled, thought Mama.

Then they were on to Mama's dress and what it should look like and how it should be cut. "Something in black I should think, black velvet, demure but spectacular as the mother, and not too showy of course," mused Mrs. Boonisby. "A little puff to the sleeves perhaps, no pleats as you would expect, but a burgundy sash at the waist matching Lila's dress to show that you two were properly put together. What do you think of that?"

Mama hesitated and then replied, "Well, I have not worn anything like that since I was Lila's age or maybe a little older, and I am trying to visualize it in my mind."

Mrs. Boonisby turned to the back room and said in a rather strong voice, "Johanna, please come out

174

here and bring that black dress on rack three. The size four one if you please." Mama waited and Lila waited and all of a sudden, a black velvet dress floated out of the back room with no one holding it. Wide eyes, big eyes, were the way of the moment, and the gasping almost, but not quite, started again, as Mrs. Boonisby looked on. Then she saw the problem and told Johanna to appear, which she did, and Mama seemed much more comfortable knowing that someone was carrying the dress and that it was not floating along in mid-air. Floating dresses could take your mind along to ghosts or goblins or other unpleasant sorts of places, and so there was some reassurance that it was just one of the invisible females that was carrying the dress and not something else. A person you could not see was one thing and Mama had grown accustomed to the idea, but some apparition showing her a dress was something that Mama had no desire to see, nor did she want young Lila to see it either.

So Mama took the dress and went back to the dressing room. She hoped that she didn't bounce into someone that she couldn't see as she had had enough startling for one day, and she didn't need any more of it, thank you very much. She made it there safely enough and put on the dress, which fit rather poorly, but then she knew that Mrs. Boonisby would make the appropriate adjustments, and she returned to the main room. Johanna was no longer to be seen but she might have been there, it was far from certain.

Tape measures were out again, the pin box flew open, and in no time at all the basics of the dress had appeared upon Mama. "Not exactly what I had envisioned, not at all," said Mama. "But nothing too bad and not uncomfortable, but perhaps a little more room in the shoulders."

This was done, of course, adjustments made posthaste, and Mama admired herself in the mirror much in the way all females in all places do when they are encased in some finery that meets their approval. Mama admired, Lila came over and admired, Mrs. Boonisby, who did own the shop after all, came over and admired and flattered as was appropriate, and so they were all set. Mama's question about appropriate attire had been answered, the dresses would be underway, and Mama felt much better because of it. One less item to fiddle with had been conquered and put away in the drawer where such things go. Thanks you's, and the pleasantries that go along with women when they are satisfied with an affair took place, and

then Mama and Lila headed back uptown to finish the rest of their day.

CHAPTER 17
ALMOST THERE

Thursday afternoon was long into the shadows when the in-house phone rang. "Packages," said the doorman, and Mama and Lila almost flew down the hallway to the elevator. There had been little discussion in Mama and Papa's house of much else except the luncheon on Saturday, and Mama couldn't wait to get her dress. They not only retrieved the dresses, but Papa's outfit was also there, and Mama, gathering it all up, made her way back upstairs with Lila in tow. Papa was not home yet and so the ladies flocked back into Mama's room where they tried on what they had just received.

"Perfect," Mama told Lila. Exactly what she had

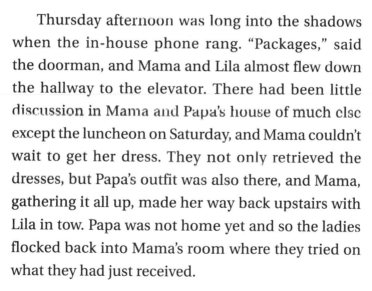

hoped for, well perhaps prayed for if she was to be totally honest. Lila had not only put on her new dress, but she was bowing and curtsying and doing all of the things that she thought she might have to do on Saturday afternoon. They both looked like young schoolgirls, which Lila was but Mama was not, in the way they carried on. "Yes, your Highness" and "No, your Lordship" and "What a lovely day isn't it, your most Revered" was practiced by both of them in turn.

"Will there be music?" Mama wondered aloud. "What do they eat and drink besides tea?" Mama asked Lila, knowing that no answer would be forthcoming, but asking nevertheless. Then once again, for the ninth time, she dragged Lila to the dining room table. Mama instructed Lila in the ways of civilized behavior. "The water glass goes here and the wine glass goes here, which you won't have to worry about at your age, of course. The small fork is placed outside of the big fork, and the knife is next to the plate with the spoon to the outside of the knife, and your napkin is taken just so and no elbows on the table, if you please. I don't wish you to embarrass us or yourself, you know, and every young lady needs to learn these things," said Mama. "Papa will be so proud of you, and I am already so proud of you, and you are doing such a nice job learning all of this," Mama told Lila.

In the manner that every mother tells her daughter, Mama went on, "You may not think these things are important now, no young girl does, but these are the things that separate polite society from, well, you know, the less polite, and they will hold you in good stead all of your life, so you just must trust me that these things are important to know."

Lila smirched, it was just that after all, a smirch, which is somewhere between a smile and a pained look and said, "Yes, Mama." There was nothing else to say, of course. Lila had long ago learned, somewhere around three she thought, that "Yes, Mama" were the most effective words that could be spoken when dealing with her mother, and that sometimes they should be used when you might want to say something else, but of course you don't. *I am such a big girl now,* thought Lila. *I can manage my own affairs and I am not even seven yet.* So, Lila was quite pleased with herself.

Late at night in her comfy bed, Lila had tried to imagine the luncheon. It came in somewhere around a princess named Cinderella, though that had been called a ball, but she supposed it was going to be like that in some way. She was secretly delighted in fact, that her shoes were black and patent leather and not glass, as she couldn't imagine glass shoes being very comfortable. Mama had made a big deal about these slippers when reading her the story, but they did not sound pleasant at all so Lila had just dismissed the notion and forgotten about it until now. She supposed that she owed Mrs. Boonisby thanks for not suggesting glass slippers. When in doubt, saying "thank you" was a most useful tool to keep yourself out of trouble. No harm would come of it if she overly thanked someone, she was certain of that.

She also remembered something about a prince and some yucky romance stuff that she had not worked out yet. But since no mention had been made of any prince, she wasn't too concerned. At her age, she was certain that if a prince was in attendance, he was not there to meet her, and that is all she cared about. She loved Papa, of course, and liked most of his male friends, but boys her own age, well, they acted like baboons or some other monkey and they were not only irritating but aggravating, and she honestly wondered how and when they would ever grow up.

"It must be like some kind of miracle for them," Lila said to herself. "One day they are rum doodles, and the next day they wake up and are not. I prefer the female version where you grow up as you go along. Not nearly as shocking." But then, she didn't know for sure and wasn't likely to ever learn as she was decidedly a girl and not a boy even in the remotest sense. She would be polite if she met any boys at lunch of course, but she hoped that her mother did not require anything beyond, "oh hello" and "how are you" to be said. Lila could do that, she could always do that, but much past that was not how Lila wanted to spend the afternoon.

Just as the table manners discussion was ending, hopefully for the last time, Papa got home from work. He came home, as he always did, and sank into his chair. Lila wasn't sure if it was just Papa or the coming home from work, but the vision never changed—he just sank into his chair. Lila had used to think that it meant he was safe, but then Lila had watched Mama pounce upon him more than once when he got home, and so she had decided that maybe it was not as safe as Papa thought. In any event, there he was in his chair when Mama announced that his new clothes had arrived. "That's nice," Papa said without too much thought.

Then Mama got wide-eyed and said, "Oh no you don't! You get up out of your chair this minute and go try them on so we can make sure they fit. If they don't fit properly, then you will have to take them back to Mr. Boonisby first thing in the morning, do you hear me? There will be no doing anything else but that. I don't care what you have to do at work."

Papa had started to protest, to say that he would just like to sit here for five or ten minutes, but the look in Mama's eye told him better. He too had been a youngster once and he too had learned the magic words. "Yes, dear," he said and un-sunk from the chair, which is the only way that it could be properly described.

Papa grabbed the package, went back to his room and three or four minutes passed. It was amazing, in a way, that men took so little time to get dressed. It was so unlike women, but then there must be a reason for this which Lila didn't know or even want to know particularly. Papa returned to the living room and Mama looked with a keen eye at him and his clothes.

Mama asked, "Turn around, will you?" which Papa did. And then, "Let me see your backside,"

which was done. And finally, "Come closer so I can see you," which also happened.

"It is really amazing," Lila said to herself, "that Papa did what he was asked without protest." But then, asking and doing seemed to be a constant part of their relationship. Mama mostly did the doing and Papa the asking, but then it could all turn around in a moment's notice if Mama wanted something or thought something should be done. It was funny how mamas and papas did things. She had seen it as well at her girlfriends' houses and there did not seem to be much difference from one house to the next. Perhaps it was that women grew up and boys did that miracle thing where they went from some sort of baboon and turned into a man overnight, and they both learned to adjust to each other as they went along. Lila wasn't too sure, being only six, but she thought this must be the way of it when she thought about it at all.

Papa had sat back down now, still in his velvet attire. Mama had appraised him and, not found him wanting, he was allowed by some sort of unspoken consent to sit down. So he sat there quietly and appreciated that he was allowed to do so. He was somewhat uncomfortable in this type of clothing and he preferred blue jeans or khakis if the truth be known, but he would do what had to be done. This was a big event after all—lunch with the Council of Elders and the Princess and maybe even a queen, and while he still could hardly believe all of it, there it was right in front of him, or less than forty-eight hours in front of him to be more exact.

Hobnobbing with royalty—now that was something he thought he would never do in this life, and meeting invisible people, well that was something he had never even thought about. It might be fun, it would certainly be interesting, and then this birthmark on Lila, whatever that meant, might mean something in the end, though he couldn't imagine what. There was no royalty in his or Mama's background, and so how this sign had come upon Lila was quite a mystery. They were just normal people from normal stock, but then so were most presidents and prime ministers, so sometimes strange things happen and maybe one of them was happening to them. In any event, Lila would always be his princess that was for sure, no matter what anyone else thought or said.

CHAPTER 18
BOULDER I, PARLIAMENT HOUSE

Usually there were street signs. In a car you could use your GPS or get directions off of the Internet. No such luck for "Boulder I, Parliament House." Papa thought this must be like what the great sailors used to do or, even better, the pirates of old that were searching for some small island. They were all dressed and they had taken a taxi and had it drop them off in Central Park, and now Papa was trying to navigate to the boulder. There were any number of large rocks in the park, and the three of them were tramping around trying to find the correct one. Mama was holding up her skirt, and Lila was holding Mama's hand, and Papa was staring at the map and trying to make sense

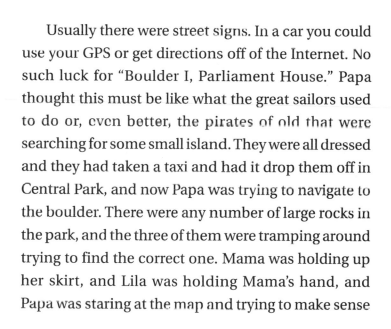

of it. Here was an adventure that they would not soon forget, that much was certain.

"If you would please come this way," said a voice as all of them jumped. They now knew that there were invisible people of course, but it still was unsettling when a voice popped out of thin air. It wasn't like the first time when they had met Ragnar, but still. "I am Brynjar," said the obviously male voice, "and if you will follow me, I will take you to your lunch. We have been expecting you. You will excuse me if I do not become visible as we don't wish to be noticed, though I am sure your being dressed this way and tramping around through Central Park will bring enough notice, but there is nothing to be done about it."

So off they went, following the crunching sound on the icy ground that must have been his shoes or his boots or something on his feet that none of them could see. It was down this path, and then left on that one, until they arrived at what must be the biggest boulder in Central Park. Not a sound was heard, not a person was in sight, and then a knock could be heard on the boulder, though the source of it was unseen. What happened next was truly astonishing.

There was a creaking sound and then the whole side of the boulder opened up, many stories high, and there was a giant room filled with very bright light. There were massive chandeliers hanging from the ceiling which appeared to be made from gold. There were monstrously tall pillars with candles set atop them rising to the ceiling's gold tiles etched with some sort of historical scenes. They stood on a floor that appeared to be made of a bluish-green marble with white veins running through it. The most amazing thing was that it was in one giant slab, with no squares at all, which made Papa wonder how it was possible. The room was cavernous, no end could be seen to it and there was a faint sound of small bells ringing in the background as if stirred by the open door. Mama, Papa and Lila were also overcome with a smell. Lilacs in the springtime came to mind, or honeysuckle when first in bloom, and it flooded their senses. The three of them stood there motionless and surveyed the incredible scene. They had never seen anything like this, nor would they again in their lives. The castles in Europe would have to take a second seat to this, and the grandeur was awe inspiring. "Well, do come in," said Brynjar, and so they did.

The room had appeared empty, just an incredibly

held them at bay in its majesty. Then, as the door to the boulder slowly closed, people began to wink into existence. First some on the left and then some on the right, and then the entire hall was crowded with people. No one spoke at first and everyone was staring at them, until finally a smile or two began to break out on the faces of their hosts. "No one will bite you, you know," said Brynjar. "You have been invited by the Princess, so do come in and meet everyone."

Papa turned toward Brynjar who could now be seen, and he rather looked like some knight in King Arthur's Court. He was tall and muscular and dark haired with a large silver necklace draped down over his chest. It had an inscription that Papa could not make out. He carried a sword at his side and not only was his outfit made of velvet, but his boots, a forest shade of green, were also made from velvet, which seemed entirely fitting in these circumstances. Papa then turned to look at Mama and Lila. He was not sure who had bigger eyes now. Lila's were wide and looked rather like teacups, and Mama's were the size of the saucers that held them. He hoped they were still breathing as they were both standing very still and not moving. They were just looking at the room as if some fairytale was being written, which he supposed it was in a fashion.

Trumpets from the far end of the room blared, and a voice like the sound of an ice flow moving was heard, "Make way for Lila and her family. Make way." The people then parted like a sea of sorts, with the middle left open for their passage. Everyone was dressed in their finest, Papa was sure. Mama regarded all of the ladies in their various hues of velvet, many with hems reaching the polished marble. Lila was just so stunned and surprised that she was saying nothing, just looking, or perhaps gaping would be more correct, as they all made their way down through the hall. Many people were tall, taller than most human beings, and many sported thick red hair though blonds and even some darker headed people were in attendance. Their eyes startled you the most, though. They were so intense that they looked back-lit by their brains, and they were large and reminded each the family of Lila's, if they considered it.

As they made their way through the crowd, there was curtsying and bowing, and many men wore swords, while some of the women had silk purses and others carried bouquets of flowers demurely in their hands. Brynjar lead the procession and kept repeating, "Make way," as they moved along. Both Mama and Papa had imagined a lunch at some long table, but this was far past the imagination of either of them. Lila, who had Cinderella's Ball in her mind, did not really know what a ball was. She did not know what to expect, but it was certainly not this.

About half way down the hall, the trumpets thundered again and the same rousing voice announced, "Their majesties, the Queen and

Princess." At the far end of the room Papa could just make out two women ascending the dais from the rear, surrounded by footmen and guards and others who protected the royal family. They stood quietly there as Papa's family kept walking, as they waited for Mama and Papa and Lila to arrive. It was minutes, though it might have felt like hours, before they arrived at the platform. They had passed hundreds of people and more marble pillars than Papa had seen in his lifetime, and while the boulder was big, it was not this big, and how this room fit in to the boulder Papa was totally without a clue. It was a fairytale castle come to life, and his family was in it. How this all had happened was beyond Papa's ability to figure out. For Lila, it was all magical. It was great magic and something straight out of one of her storybooks. She could not even believe she was there. For Mama, it was a childhood dream, a memory lost but not forgotten, and a space right out of her childhood when she was about Lila's age.

Mama curtsied, Lila curtsied and Papa did a kind of a bow. It wasn't a real bow exactly, as he did not know how to make one nor had he ever made one before, but he did his best given the circumstances. The Princess also curtsied and the Queen smiled benevolently and said, "Do come up, won't you please?" Brynjar was standing respectfully at the side as the three of them made their way up the stairs and onto the dais. "So nice to finally meet you," said the Queen. "I have heard so much about you and everyone says the kindest of things about all of you. I am delighted to see that you are dressed appropriately for the occasion. I was not sure, you see, what you might wear. I was ready for almost anything, but you have exceeded my expectations and you should be proud of yourselves."

In the middle of the dais was a table set for five. It was wooden but gilded and hand-wrought with all kinds of dragons and men in armor. It must have been very old. There were also five chairs with a butler or footman or someone behind them, Papa wasn't sure, and the Queen waved each of them to their places, with a rather smaller chair set next to the Princess which was reserved for Lila. Lila just beamed. It was always rather uncomfortable to sit in a big person's chair and have your feet just dangling there and she never knew what to do with them. "How nice of the Queen to have thought of this," Lila said to her mother. "Just how nice this is for me."

Mama smiled and nodded while Papa was eyeing the table. There were plates and bowls and candlesticks and vases holding flowers, and all of them were made from gold or silver or some mixture of both, it seemed. Never in his life had Papa seen anything like this, and he just stared at it all like it too, might soon pop out of existence. Even the silverware was not stainless or even silver, but etched gold that look as if it might take two hands to lift. "Well, hello then, Lila," said the Princess, as if this was just some picnic in the park, which assuredly it wasn't. Mama looked out across the room, and seeing no other tables or chairs, she noticed that everyone was standing around, talking politely and keeping their eyes upon the center table.

"Well, my dear, you have certainly made quite a stir," the Queen said looking at Lila. "Quite a tumult you have caused."

Lila looked at her and said, "That was certainly not my intention, your Royal, um, what is it again that I am supposed to say?"

The Queen laughed, a big fill the room kind of laugh, and said, "Highness is the word you are looking for, I think. There are other words of course, and some of them probably more correct but that is the general word for these sorts of affairs. It is all rather formal, I know, and not what you have been taught, I would guess, so any sort of word that is not impolite will do. I can see straight away that you have manners and were properly raised by your mother and father. I am surely thankful for that, let me assure you." Lila looked relieved, and Papa looked relieved, and Mama looked more than relieved as she had spent hours giving Lila instructions on good behavior which had almost been lost but not quite. The Queen then looked at Mama and said, "You have done well and should be commended, as I thought we might have to start all over, but that is not the case and I am grateful."

Mama was not entirely sure what that meant. She didn't even know if she wanted to ask because she was afraid of the answer. She didn't think it would be an off with your head kind of answer or anything like that but then she had no idea what the Queen had on her mind either. "Oh, you don't know," said the Queen as the first course was brought out and laid upon the table. "No one has told you? Well I suppose not. Your daughter is to become a princess," and it was just then that Mama fainted.

She slid right off of her chair and onto the floor in a heap as Papa rushed to her side to pick her up. Mama's eyelids fluttered and then her eyes came open and she looked at Papa and asked, "What did she say? What did she say exactly?" as Papa helped her to her feet.

Now everyone at the table was rushing over and the Queen was saying, "There, there," and the Princess had Mama by the elbow, and Lila was asking if Mama was okay, and there was a great deal of murmuring in the hall.

"Fine, all fine," said Mama. "Just a moment of confusion is all. I thought you had said that Lila was to become a princess."

The Queen looked at Mama, grinned and said, "Yes, that is exactly what I did say after all, but please try to remain in your chair while we discuss things because it makes conversation so much more difficult when you pass out like that. Here I thought I was talking to you but then you pass out. Perhaps I deserve it as I do it all of the time myself, just in my own fashion."

Mama looked puzzled and then even more puzzled and she asked, "You did say...I heard you correctly then, that Lila is to become a princess?"

The Queen nodded and replied, "The Council of Elders, both in New York and Iceland, has carefully considered the problem, and there is nothing else to be done, I am afraid. If you have an objection you may make it now, though I am not sure why you would object. Almost every female alive wants to be a princess and here is Lila's opportunity. I cannot imagine why it would trouble you in the least."

Then Papa, who had been totally sidelined in this conversation, looked up and said, "One moment please, just one moment please, as I do not exactly understand what my daughter being a princess means."

The Princess then took over and explained, "Oh festivities, and galas, and feasts, and that sort of thing. Some governing when necessary. She would be the junior princess since I am the eldest, and she would attend the occasional meeting with the Council of Elders. Not too much more than that."

Papa stared and then asked, "What about school and her friends and living with us at home and that sort of thing?"

The Princess looked at Papa and then at her mother, the Queen, and replied, "Oh yes, the details.

Well, they will all have to be worked out. By the way, when is Lila going to be seven? By law, we have to wait until seven for the coronation, so we will need to know."

Mama took over and said, "Soon, shortly, in just a few weeks. But we need to better understand what being a princess is about, you know, before we can give our consent."

Lila then jumped up and said, "Whatever do you mean?" looking from Mama to Papa and back again. "I can be a princess and you won't let me do it? What are you thinking? This can't be happening. Of course you will let me do it. I have never, ever wanted to do something more in my whole life. Even more than taking ballet lessons and equal to getting Fluffy and you must, just must, let me be a princess, please? Please, please, oh please, please? I have always wanted to be a princess and Mama knows that and so did she when she was my age because she told me so, Papa. And you both must just say yes or I will pass out like Mama did and I know you don't want that!"

The air was thick with expectation. The food had been picked at, courses had come and gone, and it was all wonderful, as to be expected, but the small item of Lila ascending to the throne hung over the table like the looming question of great influence that it was. Finally the Queen, who had been mostly silent besides the pleasantries that accompany lunches such as this, looked up and said, "Well, you two could be her regents," looking directly at Mama and Papa. "And I suppose that might solve the issue, though I had thought of giving the position to Fluffy."

Papa looked genuinely surprised, more than surprised would be more accurate, and he said, "What? You had thought of having our dog be Lila's regent until she comes of age?"

The Queen smiled, a very large and pleasant smile, and then said quite politely, "Well, Fluffy isn't really your dog, you know. He chose to live with you, and he chose Lila because of who she was, and Fluffy is not exactly Fluffy in any case."

Papa's eyes widened and he looked at the Queen and said, "Yes, he had mentioned something about that but told us that it was neither the time nor the place to go into it so we just left it there."

"Our people are an old people, and we have many traditions," explained the Queen. "One of the oldest is the mark of the Elven Queen. It comes from a time so

long past that even we don't know the beginnings of it, and the story grew into a legend over the centuries. The sign was to be found on a young girl and she was to be made queen and rule the people in her goodness and grace. This was the tale. Many people looked for this child, but generation after generation she was not found. Then several thousand years ago, such a young girl was found with the sign, and the people rejoiced. The problem was that there was a king at the time, a good king, a wise king, but he abdicated the throne in favor of this child, who was my great-great-great, and many more greats, grandmother. In any event, my ancestor. You should also understand that we live longer than humans. My family is of human origin so we only live somewhat longer, but there are those of us that live long lives, very long lives, far past anything you might imagine. Such is the case with Fluffy. He has lived a very long time."

Papa sat there. Invisible dogs not being what you thought, invisible people living in cornerstones of buildings and in boulders in Central Park, dining with a queen in Parliament House and his daughter, his only daughter, becoming a princess. It all washed over him like a giant wave. What was he to think, more importantly, what was he to do? Mama and he must talk. Details must be explained and worked out. Normalcy must live beside majesty and nobility, and of that he would make sure. Calm had been lost but adventure gained, and the days ahead would be full of all sorts of things that he could not imagine, just like the days not so far behind him.

The Queen smiled at Papa. It was the kind of a smile only given to a very old and close friend. The Queen was of some years and was wise beyond them, and she could see and feel the place where Papa now sat. "We shall all work out the details. This is a dream for our people and a dream for Lila, and this dream we shall turn into reality. As to Fluffy, when a king gives up his throne, it is a troublesome event. It can cause all kinds of problems for him and for his people. The king left peacefully after my ancestor became queen, and has wandered the world since in disguise. You may wish to reintroduce yourself to Fluffy.

CHAPTER 19

LILA IS ALMOST SEVEN

Until a few days ago, Lila had no idea what a coronation was. Now, she would be having one of her own as it was the celebration of her becoming a princess, a real princess. They had all returned to their apartment after their lunch at Parliament House, and both the apartment and her room seemed strange. She had never thought of either as small before, but now they seemed downright tiny. It was strange. Papa and Mama had attended all kinds of meetings with all kinds of the invisible people. Whatever these details that everyone spoke about were, they must be getting worked out. Details were such a bother, Lila knew, and she was quite glad that she didn't have to deal with many of them.

Papa was sitting in his chair. Mama was sitting in her chair. Lila was perched on a stool that she particularly liked, especially when she was thinking. Lila looked at her parents and thought how wonderful it was that she had them. Perhaps though, it was more like Fluffy, and they had found her. Lila wasn't sure. Lila looked across the room at Fluffy who was all curled up on the couch.

"Papa," said Lila, "will you look at Fluffy?" Papa turned and looked at Fluffy as politely asked. "Papa, I have met dogs before but never an invisible one, and now it turns out that Fluffy is also a king. Do you think he will ever let us see him that way?"

Papa mused, "I don't know, Lila. The Queen said he was to be one of your regents along with Mama and I, but I just don't know. Fluffy is evidently a very wise, er, um, dog, or person, or something, and he also obviously loves you very much. I would guess that he just might at some point, though he has never said. I guess we all will just have to wait and find out.

Fluffy lifted his head up off the couch. He looked squarely at Papa and then at Lila. "At the coronation," he said. "It has been more than a thousand years but

I am going to do it for Lila when she is made Junior Princess. It is my tribute to my young friend."

Chapter 20
The Big Day Arrives

The Ladies in Waiting had arrived the night before. At least that is what they called themselves when they winked in and then out, and in the middle they had left Lila's dress for the coronation. "Mama, why do they call themselves Ladies in Waiting?" Lila asked. "What are they waiting for? Or is it a bundled kind of thing?"

Mama looked confused. "What do you mean bundled kind of thing Lila?"

"Well, it could be Ladies in Weighting, you know, like all bundled and not exactly round, you know, not that of course as it would not be polite to say, but just kind of well, um, more rounder."

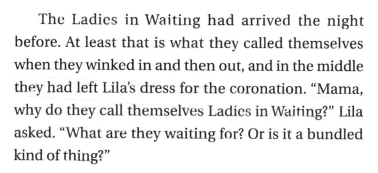

Mama grinned. Like every parent on Earth at one time or another, she wondered where her daughter had come up with that. "No, no, Lila, it is not that sort of thing it is the waiting kind of word which means they take care of the Queen and Princess as in waiting on them and not waiting for them, though there might be some of that too."

"Oh," said Lila. "I see." Well, she actually kind of saw, sort of saw, and her head didn't hurt in the almost seeing which was a good thing. Perhaps this was because she was now seven. She went to bed last night and she was six and now she was seven, and perhaps seeing was easier now. She thought of her past birthdays. They were all good ones except when Mama and Papa had forgotten to get her the American Girl Doll that she had really, really wanted, but it was not that important. Certainly not that important now, though maybe just a little more important then.

Soon she would be putting on the dress that these ladies had brought for her. Before she did that, she knew Mama would be puttering around in the bathroom putting on this and that, and then her make-up, which Papa sometimes called made-up, though she wasn't exactly sure what that meant.

Then, Papa would get a little time in the bathroom while Mama came into her room and helped her with her dress, well kind of a dress. It was a princess dress she supposed, and it was all blue and sparkly and puffed up like some of her pretend princess dresses when she had worn them.

Mama had said there would be these "repeat after me" moments where Lila was supposed to just kind of echo what was said to her. She didn't mind that so much. You didn't have to think too hard when you echoed and you could just kind of go along, which she thought she was pretty good at doing.

So the time had come. Mama had fluttered around in the bathroom. Papa had put on his coronation clothes. Lila was in her real, no kidding princess dress, and they were waiting on the Council of Elders to escort them to "Boulder II Castlerock." The knock came on time. They were expecting this one so no one jumped, and the door opened and no one was to be seen.

"I am High Lord Gudrun," said the voice. "We are ready to escort you to Castlerock. You will follow us, please."

Chapter 21

The Way In

Now it is no mean feat to follow people you cannot see. How the gentlemen got to Central Park was not known, but Lila and her parents had taken a taxi. "Okay," Lila said to Mama. "It is not some giant pumpkin with horses pulling it, but at least it was safe and it got us here." Mama laughed, and Papa laughed harder as they got out of the cab and looked for the Council of Elders. Well, maybe not looked so much as listened for them. They stood there waiting for the crunch-crunch in the leftover snow.

No sound was heard. Papa had been told where this particular boulder was though, so they headed off to find it. Finally, after quite a trudge, they found what Papa thought was the correct rock. They all caught their breath and then Mama knocked politely on the boulder. They waited. Nothing. Just as they were about to walk away, a window popped open at the top of the boulder. The well-coiffed head of an older woman popped out. "Why are you knocking? Just come in. The Princess and Queen are getting dressed. Why are you banging on the castle walls?"

Mama, Papa and Lila all looked up and stared. They had never seen a window in a boulder before and here was one more unexpected occurrence. Papa called up to the woman, "We have no idea how to get in, none at all."

"Oh, oh," the woman said. "You are Lila and her parents, I suppose. Sorry. So sorry. Someone will be right down."

"Come in. Come right in. Why are you standing about in the cold? Just come right in, please," said a voice. "I cannot be seen now. It would not do at all as I am not properly dressed yet."

Mama, Papa and Lila all walked in through the door that had sprung open in the boulder only to find themselves in a long and narrow hallway. The floor was a burnished red marble and there was nothing

on the walls except some old suits of armor that were spaced out evenly as you looked down the corridor.

"Well, go on, just go on," said the voice. "Keep going down the corridor to the end, and then you will be where you are supposed to be. Quite simple. See you there."

The three of them held hands and began their walk. They passed one suit of armor and got to the next, when Lila tugged on Mama's hand. "Mama, look at this old rusty armor. It must be a zillion years old," she said.

Just as the three of them were about to turn away, the armor, or something inside it, spoke. "I am not that old! That wasn't very nice. I am just doing my job and protecting the entrance to the castle. And that was not nice, young lady. Not nice at all."

Lila was so started that she dropped Mama's hand and slipped and fell. She was sitting there on the marble floor and she blinked. She said to the suit of armor, "I am so sorry. I did not know you were alive, much less that you could speak, and I was just talking about the armor. Not you, not you of course. I would never be so impolite and I feel terrible. Please forgive me. Please, please, please, will you?"

"Well if you put it that way, I suppose I could," the suit of armor murmured. "People don't often speak to me. Then when you did and then what you said, well, never mind, I shall be protecting you too soon enough, and so it's all fine. Just a nothing more kind of thing that can be forgotten. All forgotten. And good luck today." With that the suit of armor saluted Lila.

Lila got back up and stood up very straight at full attention, and saluted the suit of armor back. Papa smiled and thought it was one of the cutest things he had ever seen. Mama grinned at the antics of her daughter, and they continued on their journey down the hallway.

Then about halfway down the hall, they got to the Thingamajiggy. They knew it was the Thingamajiggy because the brass plaque on it said it was just that: "The Thingamajiggy." The plaque also said, "DO NOT TOUCH." It said this in very big, bold letters so that everyone would pay attention. The sign also said, "Encased here are the forces of Nature which have been tilted. The Thingamajiggy, built long ago by our ancestors, tilts them so that we can come and go as we please without being seen. All Hail the Thingamajiggy."

Mama and Papa and Lila just stood there and looked at this odd machine. It had levers and pulleys and a little steel ball running this way and that way which all whirls around some large pink stone that glistened in the light. It was a very strange contraption.

Lila peered at the inscription. Papa grabbed her and pulled her back. "Don't even think about it Lila. Don't get close to that thing or even near it." Papa knew his daughter and just how curious she was. He wanted nothing to do with the consequences of anything that might go wrong because of Lila reaching out to touch the machine. Nor did he want to take the chance that she might slip as she got near it. Whatever this Thingamajiggy did, it should just keep on doing it. He wanted nothing to do at all with the possibility that Lila, on the day she was supposed to become a princess, might stop it from its appointed task.

Papa grabbed Mama's hand and Lila by the collar on her dress, and pulled them all down the hall. "A close call," Papa said to Mama. "A very close call and too close for my comfort. Let's get to where we are going next."

Finally, they reached the end of the corridor. No door, no opening, nothing but a long blue silk cord.

The three of them stared at the wall, then the cord, and finally Papa sighed and pulled on the cord and waited to see what might happen next. The wall creaked and then shuddered, and then the entire wall opened outward and the sight was overwhelming. It was nothing they had expected at all.

CHAPTER 22

BOULDER II, CASTLEROCK

It was just a huge room. Well, not a room really but a giant dome. All around the walls were vines that were the size of your arms. The walls were made of big stone blocks and these vines seemed to run over them, into them and then through them, and apparently they popped out again but you couldn't tell which vine belonged to which other one. Then there was the garden.

This flower and that flower and big and bigger flowers that grew in excess on almost every inch of space except in the very middle of the dome. Here were two very large and sturdy trees that had grown thrones. They did not appear to be carved or whittled or whatever else one might accomplish with a knife. These two trees reached all the way to the top of the dome. At ground level were these two thrones that could only be called magnificent. The wood was highly polished, there were stately arches over them and there were wonderful pillars built into the arms of the thrones that rose twenty feet and then connected at ninety degree angles back to the tree. Then there was the smaller tree next to them.

It looked young, fresh and hurrying as fast as it could to catch up with its two larger brothers. There was a throne all right, but small and just a little fragile. There were the same pillars but they were still shooting up vertically and had not connected back to the tree. The polished look was not quite as finished as the other two trees, and the tree, at this point in its growth, could only be called a sibling of sorts.

Papa looked at Mama. "That must be Lila's throne, I would guess. It is just like Lila in a way. It is trying so hard to grow up and yet it not quite there, but there is that certain promise that it will make it." Mama looked at Papa, grinned and then turned to Lila with that special smile that is only shared between a mother and daughter, as she tugged at Lila and held

her tightly.

There will be other days, thought Mama. Other days filled with the love between her and Lila, but she just wanted everything to stop for a moment. *Please, Time,* she spoke in her mind. *Please, can't you stand still for just one moment so I can feel every single pulse of my heart and every small beat of Lila's?* Today was a day that would never be forgotten and she wanted to feel it all.

Then, the applause began. It was quiet at first, but built into a great crescendo. Out of the walls popped long verandas that were empty but for a moment, and then filled with cheering people. All around Mama, Papa and Lila, people in their velvet costumes winked into existence. No one was there, then everyone was there and the entire dome was filled with the people who were there for the Coronation. Fluffy, who had left the apartment early in the morning, was also there, standing at the very foot of the Queen's throne. The Queen and the Princess were sitting there and each and every person in the room was grinning from ear to ear as if all of the world's problems had been solved. They were here to celebrate. "This is a wonderful moment," said Papa to no one in particular, which it obviously was for the three of them.

There was a speech made by the Lord High something or another, and then the first Lady in Waiting said some words, and then the head of the delegation from Iceland made a rousing speech in his native tongue and the cheering and clapping began again and went on for quite some minutes. Then, the Queen raised her hand and beckoned for silence and the murmurs died down upon command, which is just what it was after all.

Fluffy walked over to the middle of the dais upon which the thrones rested and blinked out. He was there and then not there, and when he returned it might have been Fluffy but certainly a Fluffy which Lila had never seen. The man was tall with a salt and pepper beard and had a very ancient crown perched upon his head. His cape was made of some fur that was black and white, just the same color as Fluffy's coat. His eyes were the twinkling blue of the ocean just as the sun came creeping over the horizon, exactly like Fluffy the dog. He had a medallion on his chest which matched the birthmark that was on Lila's forearm, and he grinned and then bowed to the audience.

"I am here as I promised Lila I would be here. My
oath has been kept and I could not be more delighted

223

to share this coronation with all of you as we mark the occasion of Lila becoming one of our princesses. All hail my young friend, Princess Lila, as she comes of age and is crowned."

The crowd, who had not seen Haakon I in more than two thousand years, went wild. The dome could not contain the noise. The applause and cheers were deafening, and Lila beamed at her friend. She just stood there and beamed!

Chapter 23
Dreams Come True

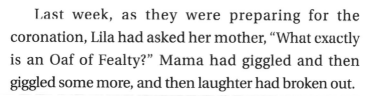

Last week, as they were preparing for the coronation, Lila had asked her mother, "What exactly is an Oaf of Fealty?" Mama had giggled and then giggled some more, and then laughter had broken out.

"No, no, Lila. It is an Oath of Fealty, which means that you give your word that you will do your best for the invisible people."

Lila knew what giving your word meant and she knew now that an oath was even stronger than that. As she sat on her throne she had sworn to this and that and the ceremony was quite long as these kinds of things tended to be quite formal. In the end, she curtsied to the Queen, and curtsied to the Princess,

and turned to all of the people and curtsied once again. Her new crown was put on her head and she made a small speech.

"Where I live in New York I could not have a dog. Then I wished for an invisible dog and I found Fluffy, er, well, King Haakon I. I hope it is not impolite to say, but two legs or four legs he will always be Fluffy in my heart. Then I was introduced to all of you, who have been just so kind to me, and then the sign of the Elven Queen was discovered on my forearm and here I am.

"I am young, I know, and I can be a little foolish sometimes, though I will try my best not to be. I have sworn my best to you and that is what I shall always give you. I am a little girl but I will be a big girl someday, and then a woman. Each day as I grow up I will carry each one of you locked away in my heart."

Then Lila sat down on her throne.

The invisible people cheered.

Lila looked at the Queen and her older Princess. Lila looked at Mama and Papa. Lila turned and looked at Fluffy the King. Fluffy slowly walked over to her.

"Lila, you are now seven. You have also just been

crowned a real princess." King Fluffy then grinned so brightly that it put the sun to shame. He then said to Lila, "Now what could be better than that?"

THE END OF THE FIRST BOOK